EARTH'S PALADIN
EARTH'S MAGIC
BOOK FOUR

EVE LANGLAIS

Earth's Paladin © 2023 Eve Langlais

Cover by Addictive Covers © 2023

Produced in Canada

Published by Eve Langlais

http://www.EveLanglais.com

E-ISBN: 978 177 384 4565

Print ISBN: 978 177 384 4572

ALL RIGHTS RESERVED

This book is a work of fiction and the characters, events and dialogue found within the story are of the author's imagination and are not to be construed as real. Any resemblance to actual events or persons, either living or deceased, is completely coincidental.

No part of this book may be reproduced or shared in any form or by any means, electronic or mechanical, including but not limited to digital copying, file sharing, audio recording, email and printing without permission in writing from the author.

PROLOGUE

Decades before the events that took place in Earth's Nexus and Earth's Magic, just outside of town, in a forest that's been around longer than anyone can remember...

"Annie!" Mindy bellowed for her best friend whose idea it had been to come to the forest at night. A spooky forest replete with creepy noises and moving shadows that made her wish she'd slashed the tire on her bike so she could have bailed and not gone along.

"What?"

The sudden reply from behind Mindy had her uttering a screech that probably woke every sleeping animal in a several-mile radius. She whirled and glared at Annie. "Don't scare me!"

Her best friend, wearing red overalls and a shirt plastered in yellow rubber ducks, grinned showing off her new braces. "If I was going to scare you, I would have stayed hidden, rattling branches and making the occasional grunting sound."

"Not funny." Mindy pouted. "You know I hate being outside after dark." Blame her vivid imagination.

"Don't be a pussy," Annie retorted. "We need to be out here at this hour if we're going to pick a blooming moonflower."

"There were some in Mrs. Kilpatrick's garden."

"You want us to steal?" Annie slapped a hand to her chest. "I am shocked! Shocked I tell you. And proud." She grinned mischievously. "I really am a bad influence."

She was, which was why Mindy had adored her BFF since kindergarten. Who wouldn't love a girl brave enough to come to school wearing red galoshes, green shorts, and a t-shirt that read, *Pie Eating Champ*? Annie hadn't personally earned that title, but not for a lack of trying.

"Wish my mom would let me plant a garden," Mindy grouched. "But no. The whole yard is a giant patio now, with no plants because of her allergies." The unfairness of it! As a witch with an affinity towards the earth and all things growing, it was ironic her mother couldn't handle pollen.

"Sorry the goats mowed down the one at my place." Annie offered an apology. She lived on a farm and had acres of places for stuff to grow. Alas, she also coexisted with animals who ate all those things.

"How much farther do we need to go?" Mindy asked. The headlamp she wore still shone bright, but she'd been binge-watching horror movies of late. She knew it could go out at any time, and once it did... They'd probably die horribly. Strung up in a tree with their intestines yanked. Dragged into a burrow to feed horrible monster babies. Spun into a cocoon for a spider snack.

"I don't know exactly how far. When I was here last week looking for Figus—" the horse that decided to go wandering—"I found them growing by the base of this enormous tree!" She held out her arms wide.

"There's a lot of big trees," Mindy pointed out. Her Earth based magic connected her to all living foliage, and though she loved them—each and every one—that love didn't mean they weren't spooky at night.

"You know, you could try asking your green, leafy friends for directions."

At the reminder, Mindy could have slapped herself. "Duh. I guess so." She placed her palm on the nearest trunk and closed her eyes to concentrate. *Hello, Ash. It's Mindy. I don't suppose you know where I can find some moonflowers? I hear there's a patch by a really big tree.*

The reply came in the rubbing of branches and the creak of bark shifting.

Mindy frowned. "That's odd."

"What is?"

"Ash said we shouldn't go near the flowers because they're by a certain tree."

"What's wrong with the tree?"

"Supposedly it's bad." Her nose wrinkled.

"As in evil?" Annie clapped her hands. "Epic."

"More likely it meant it's rotted, and Ash is worried it will fall on us."

Annie snorted. "Fall on us how? There isn't even a lick of wind tonight. We'll be fine. Do you know where it is?"

"It didn't say. But I have an idea." Mindy crouched and placed her hand to the ground. An old tree would most likely have roots that had spread far and wide. Maybe she could trace one back. Easy in concept, but it turned out this forest had a mess of roots. Too many for her to sort.

She leaned back and blew out a breath. "It's not working."

"You barely tried," Annie remarked.

"Because it's impossible. Like that time your cat got hold of your mom's yarn. Remember the tangle?" It zigzagged all around the house.

"Guess we're pooched." Annie sighed in dejection.

"Hold on, let me try something else." Mindy dug her fingers into the soil and did her meditation thing where she breathed in and out, nice and slow. With lots of help from witch forums and books from the library, Mindy had been learning how to access her power and commune with her goddess. Her mind emptied and the soil warmed as she reached out to Mother Earth.

She felt a tingle and murmured, "Hello, goddess."

Magic flooded into her body, letting her know she'd connected.

"Sorry to bother you, but I'm trying to find an old tree with some moonflowers. Do you know where it is?"

This way, daughter. The Mother spoke inside her head. A startled Mindy fell on her butt.

"Dude!" Annie's favorite new word. "What in the clumsy is going on?"

"Um, I think my goddess spoke to me." A first.

"Really? Lucky duck. Wish I had powers," Annie grumbled.

Mindy popped to her feet to give her a hug. "You do have a power. Super BFF. Always prepared and ready to help when there's a crisis, whether it be for math homework or a smelly boy."

"You'd do the same." Annie scoffed.

"We both know I would have never thought to bring holy water and a stake." Mindy indicated the backpack Annie carried.

"Always be prepared. I've got rope, a knife, and matches too. I'd hate for us to get dropped in a pit with the undead and not have a way out."

Her forward-thinking awed. Never mind the undead didn't actually exist. If it ever did happen, Annie would be ready.

"The goddess told me to go that way." Mindy pointed and without question, Annie struck off, fearless and determined.

Wishing she were home baking cookies, Mindy followed. She didn't know if her goddess guided them or they simply got lucky, but they entered a clearing with an epically large and gnarly tree. Even from where she stood, she could see it ailed via her headlamp. Many of its branches were barren. Those with leaves showed sick spots.

Annie stood at its base and huffed. "Wow. Look at it. It's got to be like a thousand years old."

"Close. More like a few centuries, which is surprising. It doesn't look healthy." Mindy's lips pursed. Something about the tree repulsed. An ache started in her head.

"Moonflowers!" Annie's attention shifted as she pointed.

Indeed, the lovely blooms had opened and emitted a gentle fragrance. "Let's grab them and go. I'm craving ice cream." Mindy wanted out of here. Something about the tree didn't feel right.

"Ooh, chocolate ice cream and pickles." Annie smacked her lips.

Mindy didn't gag. She was used to her friend's odd food choices.

She crouched and before she trimmed the blooms asked permission from each plant. All but one agreed to let her have the flower. She tucked them in her bag and stood, noticing Annie stood with her ear pressed to the bark.

"What's up?" Mindy asked as she approached her friend.

"Can you hear that?" Annie murmured.

"Hear what."

"The voice."

Mindy cocked her head and listened. "I don't hear anything."

"Weirdest thing. I'd swear it came from the tree." Annie turned round eyes on her. "Do you think it's a dryad?"

"Dryads don't live in these parts." They preferred warmer climates that didn't put them in hibernation.

"Says you. I think it's possible. I mean, look at that hole." She pointed to the dark crevice in the bole of the tree. "Great little hidey hole for a dryad."

"More like a woodpecker went too hard. A shame

because the opening is allowing water to enter which is causing it to rot from the inside out." Inner decay explained the dead branches. The tree was slowly dying and in pain. If she looked past her revulsion, she could feel its distress. Maybe she could ease its suffering.

Mindy reached out and put her hand on the tree.

End it.

Burn it.

Chop it.

Kill it.

The screams in Mindy's mind had her gasping and reeling.

"What's wrong?" Annie grabbed hold and steadied her.

"There's something in that tree," Mindy exclaimed.

"For real?" Annie's expression brightened.

Free me!

The sudden yell widened Mindy's eyes.

Annie's too. "Did you...?"

Mindy nodded.

FREE!

ME!

When the branches started swaying and the ground rippled underfoot, they didn't stick around. They raced out of those woods, hopped on their bikes, and pedaled hard for home.

They never went back to those haunted woods again.

And the tree continued to suffer and rot, until a woman named Ruby came along and finally put it out of its misery.

CHAPTER 1

Decades later...

Woe is me.

Baptiste trudged head down through the forest, shivering in his ragged clothes as the first snowflakes began to fall. Winter had arrived and he had no shelter—which was as it should be. He didn't deserve even a barebones doghouse. He'd committed a grievous crime and deserved to be punished.

But would his previous friends do him a favor and tie him to a cross for lashings?

No.

Would they stake him to the ground by a fire ant mound, drizzle him with honey, and leave him to scream?

Again, no.

He had terrible friends who kept looking for him and

shouting they loved him, cared for him, and wanted to help him.

Assholes.

You should have been an actor because you are nailing the whole mopey Eeyore routine. That comment came from his inner beast, a piece of the wolf god, Garou, that inhabited his body and always had a smart-ass remark for everything.

"Fuck off," he muttered.

You get better results when you fuck on.

Baptiste tuned out Garou and went back to his lament. What did a man have to do to get some well-deserved discipline? Why would no one put him out of his misery?

Speaking of misery, he shivered with cold.

A fire would be nice, Garou remarked.

He didn't deserve to be warm.

Then think about me, his beast growled.

"You don't deserve it either," he muttered. "We're both guilty." Guilty of murder.

How much longer are you going to whine about it?

"Until I die."

Rather not. And Garou meant it. Garou had been foiling Baptiste's attempts to take his own life, pushing past his usual control to make sure he didn't step in front of a train or off the edge of a cliff.

Damned bossy beast.

Gonna get bossier if you don't do something about the cold. Don't make me take over again.

The last time Garou had shifted and taken control, Baptiste woke naked in a dumpster, covered in pasta sauce. He got chastised by the goblins living in it because they didn't want to share.

"Fine. You want fire, I'll give you a fucking fire."

Baptiste pulled a lighter from his pocket and headed for the splintered stump of a large tree. The base of it, with its inside hollowed from rot, made a great place to dump the dry branches he snapped from the fallen trunk. Once he had a pile, he lit it. Fire shot up from the stump, the warmth easing the trembling in his limbs. He held out his hands to the blaze and sighed. If only he didn't feel guilty at enjoying such a simple pleasure. The woman he'd killed would never feel anything ever again.

Here we go on the pity-me merry-go-round.

Once upon a time, Baptiste was a good guy. He worked as the muscle for the Cryptid Authority, assigned to a division known as the Special Monsters Unit—SMU for short. He'd been friends with his coworkers to the point they shared most meals and hung out when the workday was done. A good son, he visited his mom a few times a week. Fuck, how he missed her spicy chickpea, potato, and faux bacon crumble casserole. He missed his mom's hugs even more. He knew he could show up now, dirty and pathetic, and she'd drag him inside, instantly forgiving.

Like your mom. We should visit.

Even his Pack—werewolves like him—would have taken him back. He was their Garou, a rarity with his kind, ranked higher than an Alpha because he was thought to be imbued with the spirit of their wolf god.

We are blessed.

More like cursed. It had been his wolfman shape that

had torn his fiancée apart. He might not have loved Diandra—their marriage had been arranged—but he'd liked her. She didn't deserve what happened.

She wasn't the one. Garou had been clear on that from the beginning.

"Neither was Ruby." The woman Garou had fixated on. A redhead with a power to cancel magic, she'd come to work for SMU. His first meeting with her, he'd thought she was okay. By the second, he was instantly smitten.

Bad magic. Should have never eaten that donut.

Someone had placed an intense love spell on his honey cruller. It made him shirk his obligation, chase after Ruby, and, in the end, it made him snap. Poor Diandra died because of it.

Unlike others, he wouldn't blame the curse he'd been under. He should have had better control. What was the point of being the avatar of a god if he was susceptible to malicious spells?

Gonna learn to play the violin if you keep whining.

Garou felt no guilt. No remorse. And he was annoying as fuck.

Love you, too, asshole.

Baptiste sat on the ground and rested his back against the fallen trunk of the tree. He missed his big, comfy bed. Missed his apartment. His shower. Food. Foraging in the woods just didn't satisfy.

Berries and nuts are for prey. I want meat.

His beast side was all carnivore in direct contrast to the man who'd gone vegetarian a while ago. It pissed off his wolf side something fierce.

"I'll find us something in the morning," Baptiste promised.

Your liver is looking awfully tasty.

"How many times have I said that isn't funny?" He should have never watched that movie, *Venom*. Ever since, Garou had been reciting some of his favorite parts and being a general pain in his ass.

Full moon is soon. Good thing. We're getting weak.

The reminder brought a grimace. On the full moon, he would shift. He'd have no choice. And if it was like previous times, he'd wake to his belly full of whatever Garou hunted, the blood left on his lips and tongue tasting more delicious than it should.

Meat is life!

"Killing is wrong," he muttered.

Pussy. Speaking of which, been a while since we munched on any.

"Whoa. Way inappropriate."

A wolf has needs.

"I'm not in the mood."

I swear, I will mount a dog next full moon. Maybe that cute mastiff who lives behind that pizza place.

"Don't you dare hump anything!"

I don't take orders from you.

"Why me?" Baptiste groaned.

Because you are blessed.

Funny, because it didn't feel that way, a thought that followed him into a restless sleep.

He woke at dawn, stiff and cold, the fire down to just embers. Time to get moving. With winter coming, food would be getting scarce. Soon a campfire wouldn't be enough as the deep chill moved in. Then what?

I have a task for you. The feminine voice in his head wasn't Garou but his inner beast answered, *Fuck yeah.*

Baptiste shook his head. "Can we not get excited about disembodied voices?" As if he needed more evidence he slowly lost his mind. He rose and glanced around. He saw no one but was reminded of the rumors that this section of the forest was haunted.

As he stomped off, Garou whined. *Why must you ruin all my fun?*

Because fun was for people who didn't murder their fiancées.

As the man and beast wandered away, he missed the sharp wind that shifted the embers in the trunk. The ash stirred and rose, clouding the inside of the charred remains of the tree. When it settled, a very large kernel could be seen. The seed, the size of a beanbag chair, rocked, its motions violent enough it cracked. The sides split apart, revealing a bent form that untangled and rose, the shape very womanly. Her hair, long and white. As she stretched and sighed, in a scratchy whisper like that of a branch rubbing a branch she said, "At last. I'm free."

CHAPTER 2

As Daphne stretched for the first time in more than a century, she heard the Earth Mother's voice.

Welcome back, my champion.

"About time," was her grumbled reply. Her limbs and joints popped as she rotated them, trying to work out their stiffness.

There were complications.

"You mean you lacked the right person to break my curse." A curse that was broken weeks ago, and yet Daphne had to wait until someone came along and finally lit the fire that ripened her seed.

The flakes of falling snow chilled her warm skin. She glared at the sky. Couldn't she have been reborn in warmer weather? Winter was a time of hibernation and she'd already slept too long.

The dying coals in the trunk beckoned, but that would involve getting close to her prison. She'd already spent too much of her life in that spot. She couldn't wait to leave this wretched place.

You'll need to dress yourself if you don't want to draw notice, the Earth Mother advised.

Daphne cocked her head before speaking aloud, her voice rusty from disuse. "Where can I find clothing?" And a weapon. Not that it had helped her last time. Caught by surprise, she never had a chance to stab anyone.

The Mother sent her directions via the soil touching the soles of her feet. Daphne pivoted to follow, only to pause and frown. "There is a strangeness in the air." A feeling of power that she was not familiar with.

The Monster King has returned and claimed this land.

"Do you need me to kill him?" Daphne asked. In the past, before her untimely imprisonment, she'd been the Earth Mother's paladin, tasked with handling threats.

No. I approve of his return. However, given this is his domain, and you are my champion, you will have to relocate if you wish to serve me still. I will understand, though, if you'd like to switch your allegiance. I'm sure the king would find you a position suited to your skills.

"What happened wasn't your fault."

The Earth Mother had always been good to her. When a grievous injury had Daphne on death's door, the Mother placed her into a seed. It was only supposed to last a few weeks while she healed. Alas, the same witch that injured her cast a curse that kept Daphne trapped until now. Pity the witch was long dead. Not all species enjoyed extended lifespans like dryads.

Outfit yourself, then speak to me again. I have a mission for you.

With the Mother's guidance, Daphne began to walk and quickly discovered she followed tracks in the newly fallen snow. Big footsteps dented the fresh snow and, given the falling flakes hadn't filled them yet, indicated the wearer of the boots shouldn't be far ahead. Good, because her hair might be long, but it barely covered her chilly flesh. She'd hate to go into hibernation so soon after her lengthy, forced sleep.

Within minutes, she came in sight of a bulky figure standing on the edge of the woods, staring off into the distance. As she came close, he spoke in a low gruff tone.

"Who are you? Why are you following me?"

"Give me your clothes."

He chuckled as he turned, and then gaped before blurting, "You're naked."

"And you're not." She held out her hand. "Give."

"Is this a trick?" He eyed her with suspicion.

"You talk too much." She launched herself at him, but he moved fast for a male his size. His sidestep led to her landing hard, hitting the ground, but rolling back to her feet. She partially crouched and planned her next attack.

A mighty frown creased his brow. "Are you insane? You do see I'm like two to three times your size."

"It's not about the size but the skill." She might be a little stiff and out of practice, but he had something she wanted. She pounced again. This time he caught her midair.

"Bad whatever the fuck you are."

She clapped her hands over his ears, and he bellowed as he dropped her.

"Geezus. You want my coat, take my fucking coat," he groused.

"Was that so hard?" she replied as he shrugged it off.

He glared. "You're lucky I'm a nice guy."

"No, you're lucky, because I'm not a nice woman, and had you kept refusing, I would have taken it from your cold, lifeless body."

He blinked in the midst of holding out his coat.

She snatched and had enough manners to say, "Thank you."

But did he reply with, "You're welcome?" Nope. He just stared. Apparently, some things never changed, starting with males who couldn't keep their gazes to themselves.

It took the Mother murmuring, *Don't hurt him,* for her to leave his eyes intact.

For now.

CHAPTER 3

Thank you? The crazy lady thanked him for the loan of his jacket after her attempt to maim him?

Maim? Bah, not even close. She's feisty and attractive. Garou approved.

Of all the things that he'd experienced in his life, finding himself face-to-face with a naked woman in a snowstorm was a first. Also surprising? Her wild beauty. He might have been sunk deep in his own misery, but he still noticed her curvy shape barely hidden by her long, white hair at odds with her youthful features.

Very nice. Maybe I won't need that mastiff after all.

Oh, fuck no.

While she put on his jacket, Baptiste asked, "Why are you outside without any clothes? In case you missed it, the weather is kind of shit."

"The healing seed works better without garments to interfere."

He blinked in confusion. "I don't understand."

"Not surprising. Humans never were all too bright in my time. I see that hasn't changed."

"Excuse me?"

"For what? Not stripping fast enough?" she asked with a lilt. "Move faster. Bad enough your clothes reek. Does your kind still not believe in bathing?" Her nose wrinkled.

"I'm homeless."

"And?" she retorted, his jacket fitting big on her, hanging almost to her knees. "There is a stream running through that forest and I sense a larger body of water not far from here. Both would work as cleansing pools."

"No one swims in the quarry. The narwhals can get rough." He'd gone there once and, to his continuing humiliation, got tossed like a beachball a few times.

That was embarrassing. On that Garou agreed.

"Narwhals live in oceans," stated the strange woman.

"Not anymore. Nexus has become a haven for all cryptids."

"I assume because of the resurrected Monster King. The Mother mentioned he'd returned."

"The Mother, as in, Earth?"

"As if there's any other," she scoffed. "Keep the rest of your clothes. This coat will do until I find better."

She went to walk past, and he glanced at her feet. "You have no shoes."

"How observant."

"You'll get frostbite." Said out of habit, considering he'd stopped caring about anything the moment he snapped out of his curse and realized how he'd been used.

Here we go again, Garou groaned.

She glanced at her bare toes. "Frostbite would be unfortunate seeing as how I have no intention of returning to seed so soon. Give me your boots." An imperious demand.

"You wouldn't be able to walk in them. My feet are twice your size." At a custom-made fifteen, he didn't come by footwear he liked easily.

"You make an unfortunately valid point. The only other solution is for you to carry me to a location where I might properly attire myself."

"Excuse me?"

She sighed. "Mother save me from dim humans."

Agreed.

"I'm not human."

She pursed her lips as she stared before uttering an even longer sound. "Animal. Should have known. Even dumber."

Hey, wait a second!

"Listen lady—"

"I am no lady."

"Obviously." His turn to be sarcastic.

"I am Mother Earth's champion. As such, you will carry me to a location where I can acquire less offensive-smelling clothing and footwear."

"I doubt the goddess would want you to have my help. I'm persona non grata these days." His lips turned down.

She cocked her head and her eyes lost focus before she murmured, "The Mother says you weren't at fault but since you seek redemption you should provide me with aid that I might achieve victory in my quest." The woman frowned. "Ignore that. I don't require help."

"Says the barefoot lady in the woods."

"Only because you won't give me your ridiculously large, and most likely smelly, boots."

"You're awfully demanding for someone who tried to kill me."

"I wasn't trying or you'd be dead."

She meant it too.

"Guess it wouldn't hurt to carry you. That is if you can handle being close to my unwashed body," was his sarcastic reply.

"Finally, you make the right decision. I will do my best to not breathe through my nose. Turn around."

"Why?" he asked, spinning rather than arguing.

She launched herself at his back, her weight slight enough he didn't stagger, but he did startle. Her legs wrapped around his waist and her hands clutched his shoulders. "Onward, beast of burden."

Hold on. I don't think I like her anymore. Buck her off!

Rather than listen to Garou, he replied, "How about, 'Thanks Baptiste. Awfully nice of you to help.'"

"In my day we didn't thank the horses that carried us," was her snooty reply.

"I'm not a fucking horse." He growled with annoyance, a feeling that warmed some of the dead inside. It had been a while since he'd felt anything.

Always knew you had a bit of a masochist side. It explains those ghost peppers you insist on torturing us with.

"Obviously you're not a horse or you'd have hooves and be less argumentative."

"I'm a werewolf." Might as well get it out of the way.

"How unfortunate for you."

"Are you always this rude or did I catch you on a good day?"

"I see the men of this time still cannot handle a forthright woman." She sniffed.

"You sure are a prize. I can see why someone dumped you in the woods," he muttered.

"I was not dumped. I told you I recently hatched from my healing seed after being trapped for centuries."

"Trapped by who?"

"The witch, Circe," she hissed.

"And why did she curse you?" he asked, more interested than he would have expected.

"Because she was a jealous hag. It is good she is already dead, or my first task would be to send her to perdition."

"Killing isn't something that should be done lightly. It haunts you." It haunted him. He couldn't stop seeing—

He shook his head. Nope. Not going there. Bad enough, the nightmare returned every single time he closed his eyes.

"Then you're weak. Killing is a part of life. Sometimes to flourish, a culling is required."

Agreed. You should listen to her.

He ignored his beast. "Killing people is murder."

"Not if they deserve it."

"What if they don't?"

"Then that's unfortunate for them."

Ha. Really starting to like her.

"Ever heard of remorse?" Baptiste countered.

She snorted. "What's the point once it's happened?"

"Because maybe you feel bad about your actions."

"I never feel bad about what I do."

"What if a curse made you do it?"

"Then it wouldn't be my fault so even less reason to lament."

See, she doesn't whine and cry and play a little violin.

"That's cold," Baptiste retorted.

"No, the weather is cold. Attaching guilt to actions that you aren't responsible for is dumb."

"You talk awfully well for a woman who claims she's been inside a seed for more than a hundred years." He changed the topic, mostly because he didn't want to find a reason to forgive himself.

"The roots of my tree spread far and listened."

He halted suddenly. "Wait, are you a dryad?"

"What gave it away?" was her dry reply.

"I thought dryads were gentle, fun-loving nymphs with green hair."

"That would be the Meliae. They are the nurturing type."

"What are you?"

"Not the nurturing type."

As if he hadn't noticed. "You never did tell me your name."

"Because you don't need it."

"Ah, so it's ugly and you'd rather not share. I get it."

"I am not a child to be tricked into replying," she said tartly.

"No, you're just a grown-ass woman who is afraid to

give her name, most likely for some wackadoodle reason."

"If you must know, it's Daphne."

"Hello, Daphne. I'd say nice to meet you but that would be a lie."

"Would it? Already you are less despondent."

She's right. This is the most fun we've had in ages.

Surprisingly true. "There's a house up ahead. You can ask to use their phone to call for help."

"Why would I call when I can help myself?"

"Because you can't just order people to give you stuff."

"I did with you."

She's got you there.

"Only a jerk wouldn't give a naked woman his coat in this weather."

"You only handed it over after I made you fearful for your life," she reminded.

"I was not afraid!" he blurted.

"Yet here I am, wearing your coat while you get cold."

"Not cold," he grumbled. Mostly true. This conversation plus her wrapped around him did much to keep him warm.

"Once I commandeer new garments, I shall return it to you."

"About the commandeering thing. You can't bully people into giving you stuff."

"Yes, I can. I'm quite good at it." Spoken in a matter-of-fact tone.

"You'll end up being arrested if you try that tactic."

"I require supplies, though, to do the Mother's

work."

"Pretty sure they won't care. Most people like to be paid."

I know how she could pay us. Baptiste stumbled at Garou's lewd suggestion.

"Paid?" She snorted. "In my day, we traded."

"Same thing. And need I remind you that your naked ass has nothing to trade."

"I will give them the Mother's thanks."

"Again. People prefer something tangible."

She growled. "Then you will pay them for me."

"Sorry, but I ain't got squat to give. I left everything behind."

"Could you be any more useless?" she lamented.

No. But I'm sure he'll try.

Baptiste couldn't help but be offended by both of them.

"You know what, I don't care. Here's the house I was telling you about. You're on your own now." He dumped her on the porch but before she could knock the door opened.

Seeing who stood framed in the doorway, Baptiste just about turned and fled. They were two people he knew well. People he used to call friends.

Nelly smiled at him. "Hey, Baptiste. Long time no see."

Too long, Garou agreed.

Whereas Clive nodded his head and said, "Yo."

His heart tightened. Not too long ago, he and Clive had been really close friends. He wanted to run at the sight of the pity in their gazes.

A gruff, "What are you doing here?" emerged from his mouth.

"Yvonne told us to come." Yvonne being another person he'd worked with. A seer of the future. She must have sent them to help with Daphne.

Baptiste pointed to the stray he'd literally picked up in the woods. "This is Daphne. She needs to be kitted out. She was just released from a curse and is supposedly on some mission for Mother Earth."

Daphne stepped forward, much smaller in stature compared to Nelly and yet she stared boldly.

"You are a warrior woman." Daphne nodded approvingly. Then her gaze went to Clive and her lips parted. "It's you. You helped to destroy the curse holding me captive."

"I did?" Clive sounded surprised.

"You and the magic killer."

"Are you talking about Ruby?" Ruby being the woman Baptiste had been convinced he loved because of the spell cast on him. The odd thing being Ruby usually cancelled all magic, except for the spell that made him think he loved her.

"You and she, working together, freed me from the tree."

Clive's eyes widened. "Wait a second, you were inside there that whole time?"

"Not anymore." Daphne's lips curved as she said, "It is time for me to resume the Mother's work."

"What work is that?" Nelly asked.

"Eliminating her enemies, of course."

CHAPTER 4

After Daphne stated her purpose—destroying those threatening the Mother—the warrior woman, Nelly, gave her a nod. "What can we do to help?"

"I require clothing, preferably clean. Footwear. Weapons. Sustenance would be welcome as I've not orally imbibed since I went into the seed." It had kept her fed while she slumbered, but she preferred to get her nourishment via her mouth.

"No problem. We've got pizza in the kitchen, and I keep an extra outfit in the trunk of my Jeep. Weapons too."

"Excellent. In that case, I won't require this smelly garment anymore." Daphne stripped the jacket and handed it back to Baptiste who'd averted his gaze.

Clive coughed and also turned aside. It would seem the modern age still had Puritan values.

"Thank you for lending your coat. Good-bye." She dismissed the beast now that he'd served his purpose.

"Don't leave," Nelly quickly stated. "Clive, take care of Baptiste while I get Daphne some clothes."

"Nope. I'm out of here." The big man turned to leave.

Good riddance. At least according to Daphne. The wizard, however, chased after him.

She glanced at Nelly. "Is there a bathing basin I might use before putting on the garments?"

"Yeah. Upstairs there's a bathroom with a tub. Go ahead. I'll grab the stuff from my car."

Daphne went up the stairs and took note of the strange abode. In her time, most homes had stone, wood, or mud walls. She didn't know what to think of the smooth surface with its pattern of flowers. At the top of the stairs, she noted several doors for chambers. The first one held a bed. The next, a small basin, a large tub, and a fancy chamber pot with water—a toilet. She'd heard of them through the roots that were her only access to the world during her sojourn. This was her first time seeing one, though, and she wished she had something to expel to try it.

It took her a moment to discover the silver knobs in the large tub brought water. Hot and cold. Incredible, but the magic was when she pulled a strange lever and the water shot out of the top of the wall.

The luxurious warmth had her head back, basking. What decadent luxury. When she finally emerged, dripping wet, she saw a towel, fluffy enough for a king, hanging on a bar.

She rubbed her face against it. Was such wealth commonplace in the modern world? Then again, given the fancy nature of the home, most likely a lord lived here. Who else could afford real glass in their windows?

A brisk rubbing of her flesh left her skin dry, but her hair would take much more. She plaited it in one long braid before hanging the towel and emerging. Back downstairs she found Nelly and Clive in a room with a double-armed lounging chaise and chair.

Nelly's eyes widened at the sight of her while Clive turned away. "Oh, I guess you didn't see the robe hanging on the back of the door," the other woman stated.

"I didn't, but even if I had, I would have ignored. I'd prefer britches like you're wearing." The other woman had slim-fitting, light blue trousers made of a sturdy-looking fabric.

"Then you should like the tracksuit I keep in my trunk for just-in-case moments." She handed over a bag, which appeared sealed. A strong grip pulled apart the strange metallic seam. Within were soft garments in a light rose hue.

Daphne grimaced. "This is hardly a conducive color for stealthy approach."

"We can get you some better stuff in town," Nelly offered.

"I am not going to town."

The denial pursed Nelly's lips. "Unfortunately, I don't have spare shoes, and you can't be going around barefoot."

"Then you'll give me yours." It seemed the simplest solution and yet the warrior woman shook her head.

"These are my special edition Converse. So, no. I do

have a pair or two of runners at my place, but your feet are rather small compared to mine. Honestly, you'd be better off shopping for something that fits."

"Shopping?" Daphne's nose wrinkled.

"You know. When you go into a store and…" Nelly trailed off. "You've never been shopping."

"In my time, I would trade with those on my route for the things I needed. Or strip it from those I killed."

Clive coughed. "Um, what year are you from?"

"Sixteen hundred and forty-two was when I went to seed."

The rounded mouths appeared incapable of speech.

Daphne shrugged. "I told you I was cursed for a long time."

"Almost four hundred years!" Nelly's eyebrows almost fell off her face.

"I'm aware," Daphne grumbled.

"Things have changed quite a bit while you've been away," Clive stated.

"Apparently," was her dry reply.

"Lucky you, I have the weekend off so I can give you a crash course on modern-day living," Nelly offered.

The proposition had Daphne shaking her head. "No crashing. I don't want to ever see a healing seed again."

Clive turned away and coughed again. The man really should do something about his lung illness.

"I see we're going to have to start with modern expression. Crash course is actually a term for rapid teaching," Nelly explained.

"Then why not say that?" Daphne couldn't help but sound cross because she hated feeling stupid.

"And this is why you can't go wandering off. The world has changed quite a bit in four hundred years."

Daphne might have argued more but the Earth Mother took that moment to say, *Listen to her. She will impart valuable information. Your quest will still be there in a few days.*

With her lips downturned, Daphne muttered, "Very well. You may teach me."

Learn she did. Daphne discovered that the world was full of shops where, if you offered a piece of plastic to the attendant, goods could be purchased.

Daphne outfitted herself in an ensemble more to her liking of black leather britches. Easier to wipe off blood and gore. She discovered places that sold premade food of incredible flavor, her favorite being something called a cinnamon roll made by a Nephilim baker called Reiver who used to be a cryptid hunter. He'd married a witch and gone soft, apparently, given his new profession.

Many of the changes and advancements she encountered seemed magical in nature, but Clive explained they were actually science and technology. Like metal and plastic things called "phones" that allowed people to converse over great distances.

Nelly offered to purchase one for her, but Daphne declined stating, "I have no one to contact." The only person she spoke to was the Mother, and they didn't need anything special to speak.

Probably the thing that fascinated her most? Cars, which replaced walking and riding. The speed they could travel awed, but she fell in love with the motorcycle.

They were coming out of a cobbler's store when a roaring machine on two wheels blasted by.

Nelly took note of her dropped jaw and chuckled. "Noisy, aren't they?"

"What was that?"

"A motorcycle. Harley Davidson Fat Boy to be exact."

"How do I get one?" While not one to usually covet, she practically drooled.

"Not easily since you don't have a license."

That led to Daphne frowning. "Why do I need a license?"

"Remember all those pesky laws we talked about?"

Daphne rolled her eyes. "Rules. So many of them. Don't kill. Don't steal. It's a wonder anyone gets anything done."

"Well, this rule is to ensure only those with training are on the roads to avoid accidents."

"So train me." Seemed like a simple enough solution.

"I doubt you'll want to stick around for a few weeks to learn."

"No, I don't want to be here that long. I'd like to leave in the morning." Daphne had all the supplies she needed to get started on her mission for the Mother.

"There's a bus you can take. It will get you out of Nexus, and then depending on your mission, you should be able to find another that will get you close to your destination."

"A bus. That is the crowded transportation humans use." She didn't hide her disdain.

"It is."

"That won't suit me. You will drive me," she stated. She liked Nelly and could tolerate her presence.

"Sorry, Daff. No can do. My job is here, working for the SMU."

"But there is a king now to govern the monsters." Daphne learned that the Special Monsters Unit stationed in the town of Nexus policed misbehaving cryptids. Apparently, they practiced apprehension rather than execution these days.

"We only take the really bad cases to the king. The minor stuff is still our job to handle." Nelly paused, then said, "You know, Baptiste has a license and can drive."

The suggestion curled Daphne's lip. "I don't want to ask him for aid. He smells."

Nelly coughed. Clive must be contagious. "He used to be a very clean man. He's just fallen on some rough times."

"The beast has no interest in helping me."

"He did once before."

"Because I forced him," Daphne pointed out.

"No one forces him to do anything."

"You speak as if you know him well." Daphne cocked her head. "What happened to him?"

"The shortest version? A love curse."

The revelation made Daphne snort. "Oh no, he fell in love."

"More like the spell forced him to be obsessed with a woman who wasn't his fiancée. No one realized it at the time. We all assumed he really did love Ruby. Unfortunately, it drove his wolf insane, and he killed Diandra, the woman he was supposed to marry. When the curse was broken, he became despondent with guilt."

"But he wasn't at fault," Daphne pointed out.

"Technically, no, but in his mind, it doesn't change what he did. Baptiste took it very personally."

The sorrow in Nelly's voice prompted Daphne to say, "You are still his friend."

Nelly ducked her head before replying. "I am, but only because I know he would have never done that under normal circumstances. Baptiste is a good guy."

"He's a wolf. Wolves kill."

"Not this one. He doesn't even eat meat. At least not in his man shape. His Garou is a bit more savage."

"And is the Garou suffering from the same guilt?"

Nelly shrugged. "Don't know. He ran off when the curse lifted, and no one's been able to talk to him since. When he showed up with you the other day, that was the first we'd seen him since it all went down."

Guilt wasn't something Daphne ascribed to. "This is why he's chosen to wander around and not bathe?"

"I guess. I don't know what he's thinking or doing. Maybe he's hoping one of the many monsters attracted to the area will take him out."

"What a waste." Daphne clucked her tongue.

"Agreed, which is why it might be good for him to get out of town. Get a new perspective. Get out of his own headspace."

"You stated he can drive?"

"Yes. We've got his truck still parked at SMU headquarters."

"Very well. I shall inform him that he will be my driver."

"And if he says no?" Nelly prodded biting her lip.

"I have ways of making him change his mind."

If he was smart, he'd give in before she started severing his fingers.

CHAPTER 5

Baptiste couldn't stop thinking about Daphne. What a strange—and violent—woman. Er, dryad. Whatever. She definitely left an impression.

She's awesome.

"Wasn't talking to you," Baptiste grumbled.

You never talk to me anymore. Now it's all wah, wah, wah, woe is me. Might as well just let me take over permanently. At least I know how to have fun.

"Your idea of fun will get you shot with silver bullets one day," he muttered.

Only if I'm slow.

"Speaking of shifting, the full moon is coming soon. If you're going to hunt, stick to the quarry area. No woods. You know the Pack sometimes runs there."

Spoilsport. I'm all that is left of the wolf god. The Pack wants me to rule them.

"Because they've never talked to the real you."

No time to chat when we're howling and chasing prey. You should try it, even if you're slow on your two legs.

"You know I don't eat meat."

Explains a lot about your weak nature. Rabbits only eat vegetables too. Ask me how that's working for them.

"Stop trying to convert me." He'd long eschewed eating anything with a face. Garou only had himself to blame. When Baptiste had woken up one day when he was a teen, staring into the dead eyes of a young doe, he'd sworn off meat.

Look sharp. We have company.

What?

Perched on a rock by the quarry-turned-lake, Baptiste almost toppled as he whirled too quick. Danger stalked in the shape of a curvy, hip swinging Daphne. She'd gotten dressed in killer gear since they last met, replete with daggers strapped to her side. Silver-plated daggers, he noted.

"How did you find me?" he barked. He'd been careful about hiding his tracks.

"The Mother guided my steps."

"Come to kill me?" he asked, leaping to the ground. "Can we make it quick? The Garou is being a real tick in my ass."

Not my fault someone hasn't been taking our monthly dose of Advantix.

"I have need of your services," Daphne declared.

"Not for hire."

"Never said I was going to pay you."

"Then I'm definitely not interested." A lie. He kind of wondered why she'd sought him out. Surely Clive or Nelly were in better positions to help.

"You know how to drive a vehicle." Stated, not asked.

"Yeah."

"Good. You will take me to where the Mother has need of me."

Yay. Road trip.

"No."

Garou instantly pouted.

She pursed her lips. "I didn't say you had a choice."

"Whatever it is you're planning, leave me out of it."

"Why? It's not like you're busy, unless moping and pouting count."

Burn!

The ganging up led to him scowling. "What I'm doing is none of your business."

"I see we're going to do this the hard way. Which one, left or right?"

"Excuse me, what?" he sputtered.

"Would you like me to start removing fingernails on your left or right hand? Or should I start with your toes?"

"Are you insane? You can't torture me into going."

"Says someone who's never been tortured by me. I assure you, I'm quite good. I've only rarely had to start cutting off digits to get what I want."

He stared at her in disbelief. "How is someone as violent as you close to the Earth Mother? I thought her disciples were all nice and caring and nurturing folk."

"Some are. But I am her Paladin. Her warrior on Earth. I do what her wishy-washy subjects can't," Daphne stated, looking utterly serious and sounding quite homicidal.

Isn't she the best?

"You're the Earth Mother's killer," Baptiste clarified.

"I thought that was already clear."

Like, duh. Even I grasped that.

He ignored Garou. "Why do you have such a problem with the word no?"

"Why must you make this difficult? We both know I'm going to win."

"You do realize I'm several times your size."

"I have it on good authority you won't hit me." Her lips quirked. "Strange rule this era has about men not striking women."

"Shouldn't you applaud that, given you are a woman?"

"I don't need a male to treat me differently. Let him hit me, but he'd better do it hard enough to knock me out because when I retaliate, he will regret it."

Damn. I might be in love. Garou practically swooned.

Baptiste clenched his fists, mostly in annoyance because she was right about one thing. He wouldn't hit her. He spread his arms. "You know what, Psycho. Do it. Torture me. Kill me. I don't care."

She huffed. "So melodramatic."

Agreed.

"Shut up," he growled.

Her brow arched. "I will not shut up."

"Wasn't talking to you."

Her frown cleared and a small smile took its place. "Your Garou agrees with me."

"My Garou is just as annoying and psycho as you."

"Pity I can't deal with him directly. Alas, a wolf probably can't drive too well, meaning I am stuck with you."

"I told you no."

No surprise, Daphne ignored him. "You will meet me in the SMU parking lot at dawn. Nelly and Clive have already promised to have your vehicle ready for departure."

"I'm not coming."

"You are. You just need to do one thing first."

"What?"

"Bathe."

He didn't expect her to suddenly lunge at his midsection.

Oomph.

She drove into him with far more force than expected for someone her size. The strength and surprise of it led to him falling backwards over the edge of the quarry—*Splash!*—into the water.

He sputtered as he surfaced. "Not cool!"

"I refuse to sit in close confines with you smelling like a dung pile baked in the sun."

"I'm not going!" he bellowed as he treaded water.

But did she listen?"

"I'll see you in the morning."

Before he could protest, a horn suddenly speared between his legs. The narwhal he'd disturbed lifted him clear from the water and tossed him!

Wheeeee!

Kersplash.

He landed, arms and legs flailing. Not for long. The

second watery beast that lived in the flooded quarry picked him up and whipped him back. By the time he dragged his soggy ass to shore, the reek of sweat and the grime of dirt had all been sluiced. He also had an audience.

His uncle Frederick stood on the shore, and he'd not come alone.

Fuck.

Baptiste hoisted himself from the water before growling, "What do you want?"

"I've come to bring you home."

The demand had him shaking his head. "We both know that's impossible."

"What happened with Diandra was unfortunate, but everyone, including her parents, understands you're not at fault. There will be no charges laid. Our lawyer had them dismissed on the grounds of temporarily cursed insanity."

The claim would explain why the SMU and cops hadn't been trying to hunt him down for arrest. "I don't want to go back. Find someone else to lead the pack."

"We both know that can't happen so long as you are the Garou."

"You've been leading just fine up until now."

"Things are changing in the world. With the return of the Monster King, we require a strong leader to ensure the Pack's safety."

"The Garou isn't that remedy. He's more likely to piss off the king by trying to eat his subjects."

Uncle Frederick didn't find his truthful response

amusing. "I didn't come here to argue with you. You will return whether you want to or not."

The demand explained why his uncle came with the largest bullies in the Pack. They planned to try and take him by force.

"Try" being the key word.

They'll regret it.

Baptiste sighed. "Don't make me hurt you."

"I could say the same. Come peacefully and there won't be any need to get ugly."

What was it with people threatening him today? Then again, Daphne hadn't followed through. Not yet, at any rate.

"Leave me alone."

"I'm afraid that's not possible." His uncle pulled a tranquilizing gun from the inside of his jacket. "This is for your own good."

As he fired, Baptiste dodged. However, he'd not counted on the other Pack members firing at the same time. The darts struck, and despite his extremely fast metabolism and resistance to drugs, lethargy spread quickly through his veins. He blinked as his vision wavered. His uncle had made sure to bring elephant-sized doses.

Garou bellowed, *Let me out.*

Promise you won't kill them. Baptiste knew better than to demand he not hurt anyone.

I won't be taken alive!

The best he was going to get.

Baptiste let go, and Garou exploded from his skin and clothes as he took over.

What followed was a violent mess.

For the opposition.

As a wolf, Baptiste had always been bigger than the rest. As Garou, a wolfman on two legs, he was a veritable monster, and he loved to fight.

Garou roared with delight as he swung to grab a dart gun, yanking it from Pascal's grip and tossing it in the water. Pascal charged and Garou grabbed, lifted with ease, and flung him, the splash bringing the narwhals to the surface to play with their new ball.

The other men—Joel and Lawrence—had emptied their tranquilizer guns and charged him together. Their fleshy shapes were no match. Garou's long reach let him grab them by the arms. His strength allowed him to veer their momentum so they crashed into each other. They hit the ground hard and groaned.

Garou waited—impatiently—growling, "I barely touched you. Get up."

The challenge was accepted and he got to pummel them a bit more before they slumped and refused to play anymore.

By the time Garou showed Frederick's minions the error of their ways, the sedative had burned through his elevated metabolism. The traitors to the Pack's god lay on the ground groaning, bruised, and bleeding. Not the so-called Alpha though. That coward fled.

He'll be back, Baptiste warned. *And next time he'll come better prepared.*

"You should let me eat him."

No eating people. We've talked about this.

"Then what? He's going to try again."

Garou made a good point.

Hence why when Daphne arrived at the SMU parking lot the following morning, she found Baptiste dressed in the clean clothes he'd found in the back, sitting in the driver's seat of his truck.

CHAPTER 6

Daphne sat beside a glowering Baptiste as he drove them out of Nexus. As she'd clambered into the truck beside him, she'd asked, "Changed your mind?"

He'd offered a dark look. "I need to get out of town for a bit, so might as well give you a ride. Where to?"

"The Mother says we need to drive to a place called Wyoming."

He'd whistled. "You're talking about an eight-hour drive."

"And?"

"Whatever." He turned them onto the road and didn't say another word.

Neither did she, but she did reflect on what she'd seen the day before. The beast had fought his foes with ease.

Foes she'd intentionally led to Baptiste.

It began with her overhearing a conversation in town as she passed a group of men.

"...I don't understand how you haven't been able to

track him," an older male with graying temples stated to another.

"It's like nature is against us," whined a man with a mustache. "One minute we'll have his scent, the next, a skunk comes out of nowhere and sprays us."

The male with a nasally voice added, "The one time we could see him in the distance, but a sudden fog had us going in circles for hours."

"Obviously Pack enemies are working against us, trying to make us weak," said Gray Temples. "We have to get Baptiste back."

As they passed out of hearing, Nelly murmured, "That's Baptiste's uncle, Frederick. He's the one who arranged the marriage Baptiste didn't want. He's a Grade-A asshole. Can't blame Baptiste for avoiding him."

That knowledge gave Daphne an idea. "I need your phone."

Nelly handed it over with only a single question. "Why do you have a devious look in your eyes?"

"Because I'm going to help Baptiste realize helping me is in his best interests. Stay here a moment."

Phone to her ear, Daphne turned around and headed back for the group of men, pretending she was speaking to someone. "Yes, I know you don't like meat. I'll make sure the sandwich only has those icky vegetables you like." She paused as if listening to a reply before adding, "It's wrong you refuse to do what is natural. Wolves are carnivores. You're supposed to eat flesh." Another pause. "I'll be along with your sandwich shortly. I'll make sure no one follows."

The men had gone silent as they heard her, and she

knew by the way she felt the uncle's gaze tracking her retreat that he'd understood who she supposedly conversed with. As planned, they shadowed her as she made her way out of town. Nelly drove her partway, ignoring the vehicles following, before dropping her off.

Daphne had pretended to not notice the men trailing as she made her way to the lake and the man brooding on its edge. Per her prediction, Baptiste had refused to help, and so she let his uncle do the convincing. She remained nearby but out of sight, keeping an eye on things in case he needed her to rescue him.

Turned out he didn't. The man might whine and complain, but the wolf? He was impressive. He handled his foes with ease while the cowardly uncle fled.

Just in case she gauged wrong, Daphne kept an eye on Baptiste as he headed for town in his wolf form, the four legs making rapid work of the miles. When she lost sight of him because her own two legs weren't as quick, she relented and called for a ride using the dreaded phone Nelly had loaned her.

The next morning, she joined Baptiste in the truck.

She waited until they exited the town boundaries before saying, "You smell much improved." Nice actually. Turned out the man had a pleasant musk to him that she didn't mind.

"I'd say you're welcome, but I'd be lying. Any idea where in Wyoming we're going? It's a big place."

"The Mother will let us know as we grow near."

"What exactly is this mission?"

"Apparently, there is a witch of uncommon power who has been dabbling in dark magic. While the Mother usually wouldn't care, as dark and light are required for balance, this witch's experiments are poisoning the land and starting to spread."

"Why send you? Why not notify the Cryptid Authority?" The agency governed those with magical gifts or nonhuman traits.

"They are aware, but rather than counter the witch's doing they have declared the area off limits."

"Whoa. They gave up? That doesn't sound right."

Daphne shrugged. "The Mother is also perturbed by their unwillingness to act. Apparently, some agents sent to deal with the witch haven't returned. It is possible the witch might have taken them hostage and is using them as leverage."

"If this witch is so dangerous, why is the Earth Mother only sending you?"

"Only?" Daphne took offense as she saw it for the insult that it was.

"I mean, yes, you're tough, but let's be honest, you are one petite woman with daggers against a witch that has supposedly managed to capture seasoned agents with guns, spells, and more."

"What is it with males constantly assuming females are weak? Do you think that of Nelly?"

"I've seen Nelly with a gun. She's got an affinity for weapons that makes her formidable. You have a pair of daggers. Ain't going to do you much good against something with armor or a fireball."

"Then it's a good thing your beast is good in a battle."

"How would you know?"

"I saw you fight yesterday." She wasn't one to lie. "Your uncle should have brought more men. It was an insult to your beast."

He didn't immediately respond, but when he did it was to accuse. "You told my uncle where to find me."

"I didn't tell. He just happened to follow."

"You manipulated me into coming." His hands gripped his steering wheel so tight it creaked.

"Would you have preferred the torture?"

"I would have preferred you leave me alone."

"How long are you planning to self-flagellate?"

"None of your business," he growled.

"Would it help if I said you might very well die helping me take out this witch?"

He sighed. "This might be hard to believe, but I don't want to die."

"Are you sure? Because if the witch doesn't succeed in ending your life, I might be convinced to do it."

He snorted. "Gee, thanks"

"You're welcome. I can make it quick and painless."

"You are ridiculously cocky."

"I'm not sure how being truthful is arrogant."

"It's annoying." He stopped the truck abruptly, jolting her.

"Why aren't you driving?" she asked as he exited the vehicle.

He came around to her side and opened the door, saying, "The only reason you asked me to come was because you needed a chauffeur."

"Nelly says one must have experience and a license to drive."

"Well, you can't get the latter without the former. So, let's go. Get behind the wheel."

"Really?" Her tone brightened as she immediately hopped into his seat. Her lips pursed as she realized her feet couldn't reach the pedals.

He clambered into her spot. "First things first. You'll have to adjust the seat until you can see over the steering wheel and reach the pedals. You'll also want to tilt the rearview until you can see behind you."

"I'm surprised humans would think to add a mirror to watch for enemies at their rear," she commented.

"It's to watch for cars."

She wiggled on the seat before noting, "Why is it not adjusting?"

"Because you've got to use the levers."

She eyed him blankly and he sighed as he leaned over. "They're these little buttons on the side." He stretched over her lap, and her breath caught while her heart did a fluttery jump.

He did something that brought up the level of her perch. Then he leaned between her legs and yanked the seat forward.

For once she had nothing to say because she found herself feeling strange. Tingling. Noticing the hairs curling at his nape. How the fabric of his shirt stretched over his broad back.

As he slid away from her, his touch ignited something in her that had been dormant for centuries.

Desire.

The shock of the realization led to her missing part of his instructions.

"...it's automatic so once you release the brake, the truck will start rolling."

"Can you explain again? I'm not sure I fully understood."

"Right foot goes on the left pedal. Hold it as you shift into gear," he explained.

"Shifting being that stick." She put her hand on the knob and her foot on the left pedal.

"Yes. Now, holding the brake, click it to the letter D."

She eyed the symbols blankly and had to admit, "I don't know how to read."

He put his hand over hers. "This spot." He kept hold as he pulled the lever into a spot with a symbol of a circle cut in half.

The truck noise changed.

"Ease your foot off the brake," he murmured.

The moment she did, the truck began to lightly roll. "Now gently press the gas. The pedal to the right."

Her foot tapped it and the truck lurched.

Baptiste, who'd grabbed hold of the wheel, yelled, "Take your foot off."

The truck slowed.

"Okay, this time do it slowly. You want to work up to speed."

This time, she managed to get them rolling without the jerking. The road ahead beckoned and she couldn't help but smile as she crowed, "I'm driving!"

"You are but do me a favor and don't crash."

"Fear not. I shall master this skill," she promised.

Their first full stop at something he called a red light gave them what he called whiplash. But after that, she grasped the concept. He let her drive until he claimed the roads would get busy and dangerous for a new driver.

She allowed him to take over and spent that time observing what he did. If she could drive, she could get that license Nelly spoke of, and then she wouldn't need to ask for help.

Their voyage took longer than the eight hours he'd claimed. A tire that required changing because it went flat had them waiting overly long for something called a "tow truck" that didn't actually tow them. Then there was construction on their roadway. The fourteen hours left Baptiste droopy-eyed. When he recognized the sign for an inn, he insisted they stop for the night despite being close to their destination.

He pulled a plastic rectangle from a secret drawer in front of her seat—he called it a glove box despite it having no gloves—and used it to rent them a room with two beds.

"Sorry, we have to share. Not sure how much room my card's got to spend," he apologized.

"It makes sense we stay close to one another. We can take turns on watch."

"Pretty sure we don't need to do that. The door is locked, and no one knows where we are."

Since he would simply argue if she tried to explain she agreed. He'd soon learn what it meant to travel with the Mother's paladin, just like Nelly and Clive had. Luckily Clive had proved very good at shielding. Unfortunately, Baptiste had no magic to set wards of any kind. He plunked himself on a bed and went to sleep.

Daphne allowed herself a light repose.

The attack came in the middle of the night.

CHAPTER 7

Baptiste hated how aware he was of Daphne.

She smells mighty tasty. Garou knew what it wanted to do.

Not so Baptiste. No sniffing. No looking. Definitely no touching.

His last relationship had ended in tragedy. The obsession caused by a spell had failed as well. He was better off never getting involved with anyone ever again.

Says you.

Yes, says me. He didn't deserve to be involved with anyone.

So he lay on the bed, facing away from the one holding Daphne. Unable to sleep. How could he when he could hear her breathing?

What was he thinking, agreeing to be her chauffeur?

You wanted to run away from your problems.

More like avoid his uncle and his insistence Baptiste lead the pack as the Garou. Not just his pack, though, all of them. His uncle wanted to make him out to be something he wasn't. A living god on Earth that would unite all the packs under one rule.

Because he recognizes my greatness.

You're not a god.

Close enough, Garou countered.

Whatever. Baptiste wasn't about to start arguing about it again.

Pussy.

Stop quoting Venom. He should have never watched that movie.

Best action film ever. Still waiting to see the sequel.

Never.

Moments like this I wish I'd been born in someone else.

Me too. Because then he'd have never been engaged to Diandra and she wouldn't have died.

"Stop that," Daphne suddenly said.

"What's wrong?" he asked, rolling over.

"I can hear you moping from here and it's disturbing my rest."

Hahahaha. She caught you.

"Fuck off, you cannot," he groused.

"I notice you're not denying it."

"Why do you care?"

"I don't but I am curious. Why did your uncle arrange a marriage? Were you incapable of finding your own mate?"

Admit he didn't date much? Never. "They arranged the alliance with Diandra because I am the Garou. They wanted to ensure the Mother of my children came from a good werewolf family. One with a pure bloodline."

"Who is they?"

"My uncle. The pack. They tried to organize my life. Should have heard them flip when I told them I had joined the Cryptid Authority."

"You defied them."

"Yes."

"But agreed to the marriage?"

That had been the only way to not get tossed from the CA. His uncle had threatened to pull strings if he didn't agree. "I didn't mind Diandra. She was nice."

"You did not love her."

"I respected her, and in time it might have become something more."

"Humans are obsessed with love," she remarked with distinct distaste.

"Not just humans. Haven't you ever been in love?" He couldn't have said why he asked.

"No."

"Why not?"

Rather than tell him to fuck off, she took a moment to think about it. "I never met anyone that inspired great affection in me other than the Mother."

"You've never had a lover?" He couldn't stem his surprise.

At his query, she snorted. "I've fornicated, but only because of curiosity and occasional desire."

"What about children?"

"Perhaps one day I'll find a suitable specimen to pollinate me and give me saplings but then again, I am not the nurturing type."

He tried not to react at her strange wording. "Do dryads date outside their kind?"

"There are no males so there is no choice. Now, you should sleep while you can," she cautioned.

"Night, Psycho." He couldn't resist his new nickname for her.

"Good night, beast."

He remained facing her, eyes closed, and to his surprise slept. At least until Garou shouted, *Beware!*

Roused suddenly, he rolled out of bed, ready to confront... nothing. He glanced around and saw no reason for Garou to have woken him.

Just as he readied to chastise, something tickled his bare foot. A glance down showed a roach.

Nasty. He flicked it and noticed another on the carpet. Make that several.

It led to him stomping and grimacing at the crunchy squish under his toes. "What the fuck is going on! Where are these bugs coming from?"

"Ignore the vanguard. We should ready for the main attack," Daphne stated, rising from her bed still fully dressed and with a dagger in each hand.

"What attack? Expecting the queen bug to come?" he asked, only partially sarcastic. He hopped onto his bed to avoid further grossness.

"Yes," she replied, utterly serious.

"It's more likely the motel has a problem with its crawlspace." An explanation even he didn't believe. The carpet of bugs, literally, writhed unnaturally thick.

"This has to do with my return. As the Mother's paladin, I am a visible target for those who wish to harm her."

"Are you saying the bugs are after you?"

"Did I not just say that?" she retorted.

The floor trembled, as did everything in the room not bolted down. He surfed his bed, riding the heaving mattress as the shaking intensified. The lump in the carpet pushed up, shoving aside his bed and almost dumping him in the process. He leaped clear and grimaced as he landed with a crunchy *squish*.

While he could see despite the gloom, he wondered about Daphne. Since he had the bed closest to the door, it took only two strides—crunch, crunch—to flick on the lights. It didn't make the wiggling mass of roaches disappear. Pity. Usually, things that liked to attack at night hated light.

The carpet tore open as what pushed from beneath busted into the room.

"It's the Mother of all cockroaches!" he yelled in surprise.

"Told you," Daphne muttered as the thing rotated to clack its pincers in her direction.

"Can you keep it distracted while I strip?" He didn't have much spare clothing.

"Keep your pants on. I've got this."

Before he could reply, her arm with the dagger shot out. And he meant out. It elongated and she slashed with the dagger, the sharp blade shearing part of the pincer, making the bug hiss. The writhing carpet hissed in sympathy.

Daphne launched herself at the bug, vaulting over its head with its antennae to land on its back. She sliced left and right, taking off the wavering filaments, causing the bug to drunkenly lurch.

Smart. She's confusing its senses.

When the giant roach reared to toss her off, she leaped again, this time landing in front of the bug where she darted in and did a pair of more rapid cuts, shearing some legs.

The bug thrashed in response, its intact pincer waving about frantically while its maxillae wiggled, looking to grab.

They were sliced off next, Daphne's movements precise and uncanny as parts of her elongated and even twisted, defying bone structure.

She's magnificent, Garou mooned sappily.

Baptiste would have said deadly. He'd never heard of a dryad fighting. Never knew they could do anything other than turn into a tree. Watching her dance, her limbs swaying lightly as if rocked by a breeze, her hair fluttering, rustling like leaves, her torso bending but not breaking, a tree moving in a storm, she truly rivetted.

And proved violently efficient.

We should mate with her. Can you imagine the children we'd breed?

For a second, he almost agreed. Then came to his senses as her blade, extended on a vine-like limb, punctured one of the giant bug's eyes.

The thing squealed and hissed and farted something noxious.

"You going to watch or help?" she asked as she spun past him.

"I thought you didn't need help."

"I don't. I just don't need you whining later that I emasculated you."

A statement that completely shredded his man card, especially since, despite her request for help, she didn't need him. She leaped into the air, and as she came down, slammed both daggers into the bug's head and split it open.

The bug died, spurting some white shit—on him.

When it collapsed, exhaling a stink that watered the eyes, she calmly wiped her blades on her bedspread and sheathed them before saying, "We should go. The smell will get more nauseating as it decomposes."

He glanced at his gore-spattered clothes and sighed. "Give me a second to wash and change."

He tossed the comforter over the gooey floor and made himself a path to the washroom where he wiped off as much of the goo as he could. He emerged to find the door to the room open and Daphne missing.

Oh no. She's gone! Garou howled.

"Calm the fuck down. She's just outside."

The night air proved a refreshing delight, and he took several deep breaths before casting a glance at a nonchalant Daphne who leaned against the wall just outside their motel room door.

Before he could ask what the fuck the bug attack was about, a car screeched into the parking lot of the motel and shone a bright light in their faces.

The cavalry—a.k.a. the Cryptid Authority—had arrived.

CHAPTER 8

Daphne suddenly found herself squinting against a bright light and pulled a dagger. As she lifted it, Baptiste murmured, "Put that thing away before you get us both in trouble."

"Hands up. Don't make any sudden moves," someone bellowed, their voice amplified by magic.

An obedient dog, Baptiste laced his hands behind his head whereas Daphne cocked hers, and as the spotlight dimmed, she eyed the two people making the demands. A corpulent male in a wrinkled jacket and matching pants, and a female with vividly pink hair, holding up a glowing hand. A witch, but not of the earth variety.

"I said hands up where I can see them," the pink lady shouted.

"It's the Cryptid Authority," explained Baptiste. "Someone must have called them about the disturbance."

In that case... "We've already handled the problem," Daphne informed the agent.

"Hands up!" shouted the male.

"Why?" She honestly didn't understand the demand.

"Ma'am, it is an offense under the Cryptid Enforcement Act to refuse to obey an order," the chunky fellow stated, hitching up his pants by the loops.

"Do as they say," Baptiste muttered.

With a roll of her eyes, Daphne complied, but she reserved the right to get annoyed about it.

The pink lady nudged her partner. "Disarm them."

"Why me?" he grumbled.

"Because I'm the one holding the bubble around them to prevent spells," she sassed. "So move your ass before I drop the shield and see what happens."

Daphne's opinion of the woman lifted.

The male approached Baptiste first and grimaced. "Something reeks."

"That would be the oversized arthropod we had to kill," Baptiste explained.

"Say again?" asked the male.

Baptiste simplified for him. "Giant cockroach."

"It's dead," Daphne added. "You're welcome."

The woman pursed her lips. "And you are who exactly?"

Before they could reply, the corpulent fellow held up Baptiste's wallet with all his plastic cards. "Says here he's a special agent with that new SMU division over in Nexus."

The statement arched the woman's brow. "You're out of your jurisdiction."

"I'm not here on SMU business. The attack was unexpected," Baptiste said with a shrug.

The woman's gaze switched to Daphne. "And who's your friend?"

Daphne could speak for herself. "I'm Daphne, paladin to Mother Earth, currently on a quest at her bidding."

"Mother Earth doesn't have paladins," Pink Lady retorted.

"You're looking at one." As Daphne spoke, the corpulent fellow went to touch the hilt of her dagger and got his hand slapped. "No," she added in case it wasn't clear.

"She hit me!" The man sounded surprised.

"I could do worse if you'd like." Daphne was being rather restrained.

"Listen, Psycho," Baptiste hissed. "Now is not the time to live up to your nickname. These two are just doing their jobs."

"They are interfering in my goddess's business. Surely there's a law against that," Daphne retorted.

The fat fellow blustered. "I don't know who you are, but if you think I'm just going to take you at your word that you're working for Mother Earth—"

The ground suddenly rippled underfoot and a crack appeared in the pavement by Pink Lady. From that crevice, a sapling shot up and grew, sprouting branches and leaves, even blossoms that flowered then ripened into bright red apples.

It took about a minute but proved evidence enough for the male partner to huff, "Yeah, that's good enough for me. I ain't pissing off that goddess. You deal with them while I check out the roach situation." He chose to leave them to enter the motel room, but Pink Lady remained staring.

Despite the evidence they spoke truly, Pink Lady didn't seem impressed. "What exactly is this quest you're on?"

No point in lying so Daphne told her. "To handle a witch who is deliberately poisoning the Earth."

Pink Lady's brows rose. "Wait, are you talking about the sorceress over in Palusville? The one who's turned the town into a toxic swamp?"

"You know of her?"

The female agent nodded. "The CA have declared the area a no-go zone because of the amount of people we've sent that went missing."

"CA agents?" Baptiste interjected.

"Yes, but also a few Biological Cryptid Assessors, and a Cryptid Environmentalist team. Whoever this witch is, she's not playing nice and she's powerful. What makes you think you're equipped to take her out?"

"I am the Mother's champion. It is what I do." A modest reply.

The corpulent male exploded from the inn's room and spewed on the sidewalk.

"Really, Ralph?" Pink Lady shook her head and couldn't hide her disgust.

Ralph wheezed. "You didn't see, Marissa. The bug. It's huge. And gross. And smelly."

"You know the drill. Call a clean-up crew and secure the scene."

"Why me?" whined Ralph.

"Because I'm going to escort these two people to a secure location for questioning."

"You can't leave me here without a ride." Ralph kept complaining.

Daphne couldn't stop herself from saying, "You could use a walk. More than one. A good fasting wouldn't hurt either."

Baptiste turned aside and coughed. Maybe he'd caught what Clive had?

"Wait, did you just imply I'm fat?" Ralph huffed with indignation.

"Have you looked in a mirror?" Daphne suggested.

"Why you—"

Marissa interrupted. "She's got a point. We both know you're about to fail your physical."

"I'm big-boned."

Baptiste coughed again. Perhaps he should see a healer.

"I'm not discussing this right now. I'm leaving you the sedan to get back to the precinct." Marissa glanced at Baptiste. "I'm going to assume you guys have a car?"

"Truck," Baptiste stated, pointing to it.

"Perfect. You'll drive. Your paladin friend can sit in the back."

Daphne opened her mouth to protest but Baptiste gave her a light shake of his head.

"Why can't I take them in for questioning?" Ralph pouted and Daphne really wanted to do something about his attitude.

Apparently so did Marissa because she snapped, "Have you forgotten who has seniority?"

"No," he moped.

"Good. Then secure the fucking scene."

"What if there's another bug?" He glanced fearfully over his shoulder.

"Step on it," she barked as she stalked for the truck.

"I like her," Daphne murmured as they followed the woman.

"You would," grumbled Baptiste.

Her opinion improved even more when Marissa said, "My place is only a few blocks away. You guys can shower and change while I make breakfast. Then we can chat about the witch situation."

"I thought you were taking us in for questioning?" Baptiste slid into the driver's seat.

Marissa replied only after they'd all got in and shut the doors. "No. Because if I do, you might not be allowed to leave."

"We've done nothing wrong, though," Baptiste stated.

"Not yet. I'll explain everything when we get to my place."

Daphne leaned forward from the backseat. "The Earth Mother gives her thanks and says you can be trusted."

The comment elicited a low chuckle from Marissa. "Me, yes, but you got lucky. There's something rotten going on with the CA lately."

"What makes you say that?" asked Baptiste as he pulled out onto the main road.

"Because rather than doing our job to prevent incidents, we're being told to back off."

"Why?"

Marissa waited a moment before saying, "If I were to guess? Someone wants to start a war between humans and cryptids."

To which Mother Earth whispered, *It's already begun.*

CHAPTER 9

Best road trip ever.

Figured Garou would be having a blast. To Baptiste's surprise, he was, if not having fun exactly, at least not sunk in a funk despite reeking of bug juice. He'd actually forgotten to be miserable for a bit. How could he when each time he tried, Daphne mocked him with those perfect lips of hers? Even the roach invasion had him feeling more alive than he had since the curse had been lifted.

"How long have you been an agent?" he asked Marissa as he maneuvered out of the motel parking lot.

"Joined when I was eighteen and I'm thirty-five now," Marissa replied.

"At thirty-five I killed my first basilisk," Daphne confided.

"You probably shouldn't admit that to me, seeing as how they're on the endangered species list," Marissa chided.

Baptiste cleared his throat. "Daphne would have

done that well before the basilisk population went into decline. She's older than she looks."

Marissa craned to glance at the back seat. "Considering they went on the list in eighty-seven, that would make you in your seventies or so. Nice glamour. I can't even see its magic."

"No magic. I don't age like humans do," Daphne retorted.

That statement led to Marissa asking, "What are you?"

"Dryad."

"As in a tree nymph?" Marissa clarified.

"Yes."

To which Baptiste quickly added, "But not the gentle kind you're familiar with. Daphne isn't kidding when she says she's the Earth Mother's protector."

"A fighting dryad? Hunh. They never taught us about that at the academy," Marissa mused aloud.

"Because I am the only one. Mother says the storms I weathered made me stronger than the others." Spoken with pride.

"How old are you? If you don't mind me asking." Marissa remained twisted in her seat to face Daphne.

"I was nearing a hundred when I went into the seed. That was four hundred years ago."

Baptiste just about ran them into a pole in surprise. He'd known about the four-hundred-year curse, but he'd never expected her to be that much older.

It's called experienced. Seasoned. Mature and aged like a fine wine and good steak. Garou approved strongly.

"When you say went into a seed..." Marissa trailed off.

"I was severely injured in a battle and required time to heal. The best way for a dryad is to enter a tree and let it cocoon her in a seed. Usually, I would have been in it a few weeks to months, depending on the injury. However, the same witch that harmed me cast a curse that wouldn't allow the tree to expel me."

"Damn. That sucks."

"What is most annoying is I didn't get a chance to kill the witch myself," Daphne grumbled. "I just hope something more horrible than old age got to her."

"We're almost to my place." From the passenger seat, Marissa had guided them a few blocks to a brownstone with on-street parking. As they piled out, Baptiste headed for the cargo bed to grab the bag Clive had assembled for him. He snared the one for Daphne as well. They followed Marissa inside a place that made him shiver as he crossed the threshold.

He frowned. "What the fuck was that?"

Marissa waved a hand. "House ward. It scans for malicious spells. You're both clean."

Told you I wasn't an evil curse. Garou remained salty about the time Baptiste ranted about hating the fact he wasn't just a normal werewolf.

"There's a shower upstairs in the master suite and another bath in the guest room." Marissa indicated the staircase. "I've got a large hot water tank so you can both sluice off at the same time. I'll be in the kitchen when you're done."

As he and Daphne headed to the second level, he couldn't help casting a glance back down.

"Why are you acting as if you expect an attack?" Daphne asked point blank.

"Because she's being too nice." The agent had gone from holding a weapon on them and threatening them to inviting them into her home.

"The Mother says Hekate has told this witch of hers to give us any aid we require. She can be trusted."

"Hekate is the goddess of magic," he stated, trying to recollect his lessons on the gods of Earth. There were many. Too many for a man with a piece of one inside to really bother about.

"It's a misnomer as all the gods have magic. But Hekate's disciples tend to have access to more types of it as opposed to being restricted to just one element. From what I've sensed thus far, Hekate must favor Marissa as the wards on her home are strong. We can rest easy here. My enemies won't be able to track us."

They reached the top of the stairs, and he pointed her to the double doors. Mostly likely the master suite. "You can use the bathroom in Marissa's room. I'll use the guest one."

It didn't take him long to shed the ruined clothes and bathe the stink from his skin. Once dressed, he headed downstairs with his ruined garments and had to apologize as he entered the kitchen redolent with yummy smells. "Sorry for bringing the smelly stuff in here. I didn't know where to toss them since they're garbage."

Marissa pointed to a door with a spatula. "Garbage

can is outside. Just be sure to lock the lid. The raccoons keep bypassing my repelling spells."

"Are you sure it's raccoons?" he asked after he'd disposed of the soiled items and returned inside. "Smells like goblins to me."

"Those little buggers." She waved her flipping implement. "That must be why my spell isn't working."

"A friend of mine deals with their goblins by giving them scraps and buying the occasional treats."

Marissa's nose wrinkled. "Why would they feed goblins?"

"Because they can actually be good at getting rid of all organic waste, plus they provide security. They're fiercely territorial and will protect the property."

"Hunh. That's an interesting idea. I might have to try that. Thanks." She smiled at him, and it was as he replied in kind that Daphne walked in, dewy-faced, her hair pulled back in a braid.

She scowled as her gaze bounced between them.

She's jealous. Understandable. You should reassure her she has nothing to worry about.

How could she be jealous? They had only barely met, and she certainly had no interest in him like that.

And people think I'm the dumb one.

"Hungry?" Marissa queried aloud as she turned back to the stove.

"Yeah, but I gotta ask, do you always cook in the middle of the night?" Because at not even four, it was still dark outside.

"I keep weird hours." Marissa shrugged as she ladled

scrambled eggs onto a plate and pushed some buttered toast at them.

When she offered him bacon from a pile on a plate, he refused. "Sorry, I don't eat meat."

Marissa froze. "Oh shit. I didn't even think to ask. Do you need, like, fruits or veggies?"

"I'm vegetarian so eggs and toast are fine."

"He's weird," Daphne stated. "But I see it as more bacon for us." She grabbed several strips.

As they ate, the discussion began.

"What can you tell us about this witch over in Palusville?" he asked, dipping his bread into the eggs before biting.

"She's been around for a while but didn't raise any flags. She was registered, and as far as the CA knew, and not causing any harm. She didn't appear to be using her magic to do much at all. No store selling products. No adverts for her services."

"When did the problems start?" Baptiste queried.

"That's been harder to pinpoint. Palusville has always had a transient population. It's a little town in the middle of nowhere that would have died years ago but for the fact it's right off a major transport route. It mostly services truckers and those passing through. It took a while before the disappearances began forming a pattern that involved all last known sightings of the missing people being in, or around, Palusville."

"This witch is sacrificing them?" Daphne asked in between inhaled bacon bites.

He still couldn't wrap his head around the fact a dryad ate meat. Shouldn't they be the ultimate vegans?

Marissa rolled her shoulders. "I don't know what she's doing. The CA has classified the file on her. Only those with authorization can get a look at it."

"Surely someone is investigating her. You said agents went missing," Baptiste pointed out.

Marissa shook her head. "Nope. Not anyone from our office, and it's the closest CA hub. Even worse, they've not put out any kind of warning. People are still travelling through that area, and not all of them are making it to their final destination. Concerned families have been contacting our office and getting the runaround."

"You mentioned you worried we'd be detained. Why?" Baptiste cleaned his plate of eggs with his last bit of toast.

"I don't know if they would have, but given all the secrecy and oddness about my CA office's dealing with Palusville, I think it very possible they might have done something to impede your quest had they learned of it."

"The Mother would not have been pleased." Daphne pursed her lips.

"Hence why we're here instead of at the precinct." Marissa leaned back in her chair with her mug of coffee. "So what's your plan?"

"Go to Palusville, locate the witch, put a stop to her poisoning of the Earth." Daphne had a simple answer.

"You're not planning to arrest her, are you?" Marissa concluded.

Without any hesitation, Daphne replied, "The Mother wants the threat eliminated."

Marissa's gaze shifted to Baptiste. "And you're okay

with that? I thought the SMU was about capturing and bringing in the monsters."

He hedged. "Technically, I'm not on active duty. A personal matter forced me to take a leave of absence. I'm basically just a chauffeur."

"I don't need his help handling a witch," Daphne scoffed.

A chime sounded and Marissa stiffened.

"What is that?" he asked, rising from his seat.

We've got company, Garou stated before Marrisa could reply.

"Someone's on the roof." Her expression grim, she set down her mug.

His gaze went upward as if he could see through the ceiling. "Could it be a bird or raccoon?"

"The spell is detecting two humanoid figures." Marissa's gaze went out of focus. "Three more have just come over the fence from the alley in the back. And a pair of vans just parked out front with another half dozen people."

"Any idea who?"

"Agents from my office." Her lips flattened. "I think Ralph ratted us out."

Daphne stood and pulled her daggers, leading to Baptiste growling, "You can't kill CA agents." He then glanced at Marissa. "I assume they're here to bring us in for questioning."

"Maybe. It's odd they didn't try contacting me first." Her phone sat on the table and showed no notifications when she tapped the screen to wake it. "Let me go outside and chat with them. Maybe it's a misunderstanding and they think you've taken me hostage."

Marissa left them, and Baptiste moved from the kitchen to the dark living room where he could watch from the window, keeping his bulk to the side in case of snipers. He observed as Marissa emerged and confronted a woman in a pantsuit standing alongside Ralph. It seemed Marissa had been correct about the rat.

The good, quality windows kept him from hearing anything, but it did appear as if Marissa argued. Her hands waved and when Ralph dangled handcuffs, she slapped at them.

Two more agents moved in, boxing Marissa. Their hostess kept protesting but didn't fight as Ralph cuffed and loaded her in the back of a van. That didn't bode well if they were arresting one of their own.

I won't let them take us alive! Garou promised.

We're not fighting the good guys, Baptiste replied with a grimace. "Looks like we're about to be arrested."

"I have done no crime." Daphne had her daggers palmed.

"No, we haven't, so before you go on a killing spree, maybe we could try talking to them."

She eyed him. "Do you really think they'll listen to us when they didn't listen to one of their own?"

She's smart, that one.

She was, and Baptiste agreed with her assessment. Still, fighting against the office he'd held in high regard for so long stuck in his craw.

An amplified message suddenly came booming

through the walls. "This is the Cryptid Authority. Come out with your hands up."

They didn't say paws. Garou's sly rejoinder.

"There aren't that many," Daphne noted.

"If you fight them, you'll have the entire Cryptid Authority coming against you."

"They would defy the Mother?" she asked in shock.

"They don't obey gods, but serve the people." Part of the oath.

"I don't have time to be detained," she complained. "I have a mission to complete."

"Most likely they'll take us in, ask a few questions, and release us in a few hours for lack of cause." He wasn't exactly lying. Usually, in the case of a non-crime, that would be the norm. But Marissa seemed to think her office might not be exactly following the rules.

"And if they don't?" Daphne countered.

"Then I guess you'll be justified in using force to escape."

Let there be carnage!

Baptiste hoped not. He only had one more clean outfit.

CHAPTER 10

DAPHNE READIED HERSELF TO FIGHT ONLY TO HESITATE AT THE Earth Mother's command. *Don't fight the arrest.*

While obedient, she did question. *What about my mission?*

Despite how it might seem, this will actually help you to achieve your goal.

She had to wonder how but trusted the Mother. *What if they try to harm me?*

Then do what you must to stay alive.

"Ready?" Baptiste asked with his hand on the door.

"Yes. And you'll be glad to know I won't hurt them so long as they don't harm me." She reluctantly re-sheathed her daggers.

"Fair enough." He opened the door, but she stepped out first to shouts of, "Hands in the air. Drop your weapons."

"Which is it? If I do one, I can't do the other," was her cheeky reply as she noted the many guns—and glowing hands—aimed her way.

"Just put your hands on your head," the woman in charge barked. "Any other move and we will use force."

"Promise?" Daphne dared them to try because then she wouldn't be bound by the Mother's demand. She did obey, though, and put her hands atop her head. As if that would slow her down if she had to act.

Amateurs.

Someone approached with heavy-looking manacles of iron. Pure iron. The one thing a dryad detested because it impeded her ability to talk to the Mother.

It's okay, my champion. Let them think you are cooperating.

Think indeed. These idiots obviously had no idea what she was capable of. Then again, they'd never met a dryad like her.

The Mother's reassurance didn't stop her grimace as they clamped the cold metal around her wrists and confiscated her daggers. The instant loss of contact with the Earth jarred, especially so soon after her release. She'd spent four hundred years cut off from the Mother, but it wouldn't kill her to do it again if it served the mission.

As Ralph—the man she should have slapped when she got a chance—herded her towards the vehicle, Baptiste emerged from the house, hands laced on his head. Offering himself up meekly. Peacefully.

The agents didn't care.

He bellowed as a net of silver dropped on him from above, encasing his entire body.

So much for not fighting arrest. The big man thrashed and pushed at the webbing, horror and fear twisting his expression. The beast didn't like being nullified.

"Hold still!" yelled the woman. "Where's the silver cuffs?"

Someone trotted over and Baptiste held still, but not easily. She could see the trembling in his frame. He winced as the silver cuffs went around his wrists. They also added a set to his legs attached by a long chain that allowed him to do a shuffling walk that jingled because of all the silver.

"This isn't necessary," he grumbled.

"We don't take chances with murderers," was the woman's cold reply.

"Those charges were dropped," he retorted.

"We'll see about that," the woman stated. "Load them up."

Daphne and Baptiste were placed in the back of the van with a glowering Marissa. The doors slammed shut and a spell dropped over the vehicle, muffling outside sound.

Marissa muttered, "Sorry. If I'd known Ralph would be such a snitch, I wouldn't have taken you back to my place."

"Not your fault," Baptiste replied through a tight jaw. "Did they say what we're being arrested for?"

"I asked and was told it wasn't my business. I said fuck yeah it was, since you put me in cuffs. The boss said he was proving a point about my conduct." Marissa's lips pursed. "Something's not right about this. They came way too well prepared. How did they know to bring iron cuffs for a dryad and silver for a werewolf?

Not to mention the silver netting isn't from our armory."

Daphne's lips pursed. "Someone warned them we'd be coming."

"They didn't just warn, they equipped them," Baptiste growled. "And I'll bet I know who."

"Your uncle must have contacted the local authority." Daphne understood right away. "But how did he know where we were going?"

At that query, he shrugged. "No idea, but I should have known he wouldn't give up so easily. I'm sorry. Seems like this mock arrest might be more about me than you."

"Don't be so sure about that," Marissa interjected as the van came to a halt.

"Meaning what?" Baptiste questioned.

"The first thing the boss asked me was if I had a dryad with white hair inside. She knew about Daphne."

Baptiste glanced at Daphne. "Did my uncle know what you were?"

She shook her head. "We never interacted."

"Could it be scent that gave her away?" Marissa asked.

Before anyone could reply, the doors to the back of the van opened. An agent in full body armor pointed at Daphne. "You. Come with me."

Rather than move she asked, "Why?"

"Do as you're told," he snapped.

"Where are you taking her?" Baptiste surged to his feet but had to hunch in the confined space.

"None of your business."

Marissa took a softer tone as she said, "What's going on, Dylan? I thought we were all going to headquarters."

The guy glanced sideways before uttering a whispered, "You guys are, but the boss lady says the dryad is going elsewhere. There's an unmarked sedan waiting with some dude I've never seen before driving it."

"You know this isn't right," Marissa argued.

"It's okay," Daphne stated, shuffling to the open door. "The Mother knew and seemed to think this would advance my quest."

"Now might be a good time to pull your psycho shit," Baptiste advised.

"I'll be okay, Beast. Try and steer clear of your uncle while I deal with matters." Daphne hopped to the ground, eschewing the offered hand.

Outside, the sky lightened as dawn prepared to break. Her favorite time of day. Sun was life and its warm touch always brought joy.

Daphne needed no prompting to walk to the parked car with the woman in charge standing by it, but she did stop to eye her and say, "The Mother sees you and knows what you've done."

The woman only showed the faintest of reactions before sneering. "And yet she does nothing while her so-called paladin is taken into captivity."

"The Mother gives me autonomy to act. Can you say the same of whomever you're obeying?"

The mark hit, and the woman's eyes flashed with anger. "Get in the car."

"Where am I going?"

"There's a witch who wants to see you."

"Really?" Daphne's expression brightened. "Why didn't you say so?" She hopped in and sat before saying impatiently, "Close the door that we might get on our way. I am eager to complete my mission."

The door slammed shut and the car lurched into motion, the driver remaining silent, which suited her fine. They drove long enough that the morning sun had fully crested before they pulled to a stop in a gas station long vacant. The pumps that provided fuel were missing their hoses and weeds grew through the tarmac and the windows of the building were covered with boards.

Despite its abandonment, another vehicle was parked, and from it emerged two people, disheveled and hollow-eyed. A man and a young woman.

Her driver opened the door for Daphne and ordered her, "Get out."

It appeared to be an exchange. Daphne for the pair.

She strutted without qualm to the other vehicle, the driver a brutish fellow with a patch over an eye and a scent that displeased. Acrid and unpleasant.

He said nothing as she slid into the rear seat. She tried to ask questions as he drove—"Where are we going?" "Who do you work for?" "Is it far?"—but he remained silent.

Given his lack of communication, she napped. Might as well be well rested for her arrival. She woke when the vehicle jostled, having left smooth pavement for a rutted path, pitted and muddy in spots. The foliage grew increasingly dense, but not in a healthy way. She spotted the signs of rot and decay as leaves that should have been green instead showed hints of black mold and even white fungal spores. The air, heavy with moisture, reeked of death.

She'd found the area that concerned the Mother.

The car stopped by a cottage. A quaint thing that wouldn't have been out of place in her time with its river stone walls and thatched roof.

Not so quaint? The pile of skulls surrounding a steaming cauldron, the fumes of it a sickly green.

She'd been delivered to the home of the witch. Excellent, although she did wonder why the witch had requested her.

"Get out," the one-eyed man ordered.

Though still cuffed, she was able to open her own door. She slid out of the vehicle which sped off, leaving her stranded. She'd worry about leaving this place once she dealt with the witch.

Speaking of whom, the cottage door opened.

A woman appeared, her light blonde hair pulled into a bun atop her head, her trim figure wearing modern clothing, but her face…

Daphne's jaw dropped as the face that had haunted her in the seed smirked at her surprise.

"Well, well, if it isn't the Mother's champion back from her long sojourn."

A taunt that barely registered as Daphne grappled with one fact: Circe was still alive!

CHAPTER 11

WHEN ARE WE GOING TO FIND HER? GAROU KEPT ASKING.

Baptiste had no answer. But he was getting pissed.

The CA agents had brought him and Marissa to their precinct, a modern building made of cement poured over iron rods. Great for disrupting most magic. They directed him to a cell, still manacled in silver, although they did remove the net from him.

Fucking shit burns. Garou did not like their treatment thus far and Baptiste couldn't blame him. First off, they'd done nothing wrong. Killing a giant roach? Should have gotten them a medal not a ride in the paddy wagon.

Secondly? While he might not have agreed with his uncle's meddling, the fact remained the murder charges had been dropped. They had no cause to bring him in for that.

Third, the silver net they'd used showed forethought and collusion with a pack. Because usually when a werewolf misbehaved—a.k.a. got violent and started attacking humans—it wasn't the CA that handled it, but the Pack for that area. It should be noted, the Pack was much stricter and more unforgiving.

Fourth… where the fuck was Daphne?

"This is bullshit!" Marissa cursed as she paced the cell across from him. "I'm a fucking agent who's committed no crime and yet they've locked me up like a criminal and hobbled my power with not even a hint of why."

"Sorry we got you in trouble." At this point, Baptiste couldn't tell if it was Daphne's mission, his Garou status, or both that led to this happening.

"Don't apologize. I told you something stank, and this just proves it." Marissa glared at her bars as if she could laser them.

"Any idea where they might have taken Daphne? Is there another set of cells?"

"No."

"Maybe she's being questioned."

At his suggestion, Marissa shook her head. "I doubt it. Her being removed mid-transport isn't normal."

She's in danger. He didn't need Garou pointing it out to come to that conclusion.

Agitation had him raking fingers through his hair. "We have to get out of here. When is someone going to come talk to us?"

"Should have already happened. Normally, we question first, then put a person in a cell if they deserve it. This entire fiasco is completely backwards."

"I don't know how long I can sit here doing nothing." Worry over Daphne had him pacing, and despite the silver cuffs, Garou seethed and pulsed. It should be noted, silver worked on werewolves, but he hadn't heard of it being tested on a Garou. Could it be that carrying the wolf god would allow him to bypass the restriction that prevented any kind of shifting while in contact with silver?

I'm stuck. That answered that question.

"Can't do much until they deign to finally speak to us," Marissa grumbled as she paced her cell. She paused as the door at the far end buzzed and clicked, giving entry to an agent.

Not just any agent. The rat himself. Ralph.

The smug fuck waddled to stand in front of Marissa's cage.

"You have a lot of nerve," she huffed. "Snitching on your partner."

"How was it snitching? You said you were taking them in for questioning. When you didn't show at headquarters, I got worried," the smirking fuck lied.

"Worried my ass," she hotly retorted. "You didn't call or text. Didn't knock on my door. You showed up with a SWAT team!"

"What else could I do when I realized you were associating with a violent criminal?"

"Those charges were dropped," Baptiste argued.

"Guess our office didn't hear." More lying by the asshole who didn't deserve to wear a badeg.

"Well, you know now. Release us."

"No can do." Ralph smirked. "Boss wants to know what you were doing with them in your house."

"We were having a chat over breakfast. You know the meal you have twice before lunch," Marissa tartly tossed.

Ralph bristled. "No need to be a bitch."

It led to Baptiste growling. "Watch your mouth."

The fat fuck whirled and had the nerve to smirk. "Or what? You're bound in silver and in a cell. What are you going to do?"

Let me eat his face.

He just might if Ralph kept pushing his buttons.

"What are you holding us on? What are the charges?" Marissa demanded.

"No charges. Although the boss does want to know why you were colluding with them."

"There was no collusion. Jesus fucking Christ, Ralph. Use your head for something other than a pie stuffing hole."

"With that kind of attitude, you won't be getting out any time soon."

"This is harassment. I'm going to complain." She jabbed her finger at Baptiste. "And he'll probably sue. You know we're not allowed to get involved in Pack matters."

"We aren't."

"Yet I'm in a cage," Baptiste countered.

"Only until your ride arrives." Ralph jerked a thumb at Baptiste. "Once he's on his way with his uncle, maybe if you're nice, I'll let you go."

At the mention of his uncle, Baptiste spat, "I am not a child to be remanded into the custody of a family member. If you're not charging me, then I know my rights. I demand to be released at once." The firm request emerged in a growl.

"Can't do that. Apparently, your Pack reported you

mentally unstable and missing. Since they had a feeling you might be heading this way, they couriered us the net."

"I am not unstable. Nor am I missing."

"If you say so. Don't care. You're a werewolf which means you're a Pack problem. Within the hour, you'll be out of our hands."

"And Daphne?" he asked, keeping his voice low and calm despite the bristling Garou within.

"Off to meet with someone," Ralph only partially answered.

"Who?" he snapped.

"Guess you'll find out soon enough." The fucker had the nerve to look blasé as he said, "The witch in Palusville."

"What?" he roared, causing Ralph to stagger back. "Why the ever-loving fuck would you hand over a civilian to someone engaging in criminal activity?"

"Because the witch contacted the boss and offered two of our agents back in exchange for the dryad."

"And she agreed?" Marissa sounded shocked.

"Boss didn't have a choice if she wanted them returned."

"She did have a choice. She could have done her fucking job and taken out the witch!" Marissa countered.

"The whole problem is no one can get near Circe. So this was the best way to get our people back."

Baptiste went very still. "What did you call the witch in Palusville?"

"Circe."

The name sounded familiar, and it took a moment to

remember why. Circe was the name of the person who'd cursed Daphne centuries ago. Could be a coincidence. "How old is she?"

"Why does it matter?"

"How fucking old?" Baptiste shouted, gripping the bars hard enough they groaned.

Ralph took a step back and frowned. "I don't know. But rumor has it she's been squatting there more than a century."

The knot in his stomach tightened at the realization Daphne might be at the mercy of her greatest enemy. It led to him seething, and an agitated Garou pulsed within, making the silver shackling him burn fiercely where it touched skin. But he didn't care.

He wrenched at the bars as he hissed, "You fucking bastard. How dare you act like it's not a big fucking deal. You traded a woman's life to a criminal."

"Not a woman. A nymph. A brainless fucking plant." Ralph insulted Daphne and it made something snap inside Baptiste.

"She's smarter than you, dough boy." Baptiste pulled at the cage holding him and heard a satisfying creak.

Ralph retreated with wide eyes, his ass hitting the bars of Marissa's cell. Her arm emerged and wrapped around his throat, choking him off. Ralph struggled and clawed at her arm but Marissa didn't relent until he slumped, unconscious.

"Two-timing fucker," Marissa muttered. "The only reason he hasn't been fired is because his daddy used to be a hero." She dropped to her knees and searched the snoring body.

"He doesn't have the cell block keys," Baptiste remarked. Those remained in the anti-magic Faraday-type box by the door.

"No, but he does have the cuff ones." She lifted the little keys triumphantly. In seconds, she'd shed her magic-disrupting manacles and was groping the lock to her cell.

"You can't do magic inside CA buildings," Baptiste noted.

"Not entirely true. For most it's impossible because of safeguards, but I'm not most people. Now that the cuffs are off, the magic is muffled but still there." Her forehead creased as she concentrated. The lock glowed and clicked. "Lucky for us, I don't need much to open doors." She crossed to his cell and unlocked his cage. The silver manacles dropped at her touch.

Freedom, Garou crowed.

Ralph groaned on the floor.

Now can I eat him?

"We don't have time," he murmured.

"Agreed," she replied, thinking he spoke to her. "We better go before this uncle of yours arrives."

"Go how? We're in the heart of the CA building. We can't exactly walk out."

The corner of her mouth lifted. "Wanna bet? First, we need a distraction."

"Going to pull the fire alarm?" He wasn't entirely joking. It worked in movies.

"No, because that just evacuates the building, meaning we'd have guards in here looking to drag us out. We need something that will keep them too busy to think about us and I know just the thing." She didn't head for the door Ralph came through but the one on the opposite end.

Given Ralph was starting to stir, Baptiste grabbed hold and heaved him into his cell, the clang of the door shutting very satisfying.

"Does Ralph have magic?" he asked.

"Not enough to do anything. His claim to fame is he can move small objects. Very small," she tossed over her shoulder as she fiddled with the door.

"What's in that room?" he asked as he neared to see her undoing a series of locks, some of them mechanical, others bound by spells.

"Illegal cryptids waiting for shipment back to their countries."

"Should you be releasing them? I assume they're dangerous given that you've got them locked away."

She cast a grin in his direction. "Not dangerous so much as pesky. Also, very hard to catch. Leprechauns are tricky creatures. Mischievous and vindictive to those who wrong them. Say, like the agents who brought them in," she said as she swung open the door.

A little man with red hair and a matching beard in a bright green suit stood waiting, looking benign. "Fair witch, how are you this fine day?"

She crouched. "I'm excellent, Rufus. But I'd like to exchange favors."

"Speak your bargain, milady." He tucked his diminutive hands behind his back.

Baptiste glanced past him to see other figures in green eyeing the conversation. All male. Eight in total.

"In exchange for me releasing you and your band, I need a distraction of epic proportion that my friend and I might slip away unnoticed."

Rufus had a smile bigger than his head. "That can be arranged with pleasure, fair witch."

"Once you escape this room, you're on your own," she warned. "I can't guarantee they won't catch you."

"Worry not about us, we have no intention of being snared again."

"Then you might want to avoid rainbows in the future."

The statement caused Rufus to scowl. "We need to work on our weakness. But it's hard to resist looking for the treasure we've lost." Leprechauns claimed to have come to Earth via a rainbow road from a place of endless bounty. They'd been trying to return ever since, only the rainbows they'd been trying to follow turned out to be duds.

Marissa held out her hand, sliding it through a barrier that shimmered, which explained why the little men hadn't fled already. "So we have a bargain?"

A tiny hand shook her finger. "Agreed."

"Excellent." She stood before waving a hand. "Good luck."

"Screw luck," yelled a tiny voice. "Let's go fuck up some shit, boys."

The small horde raced past, a bright blur of green that had to pause at the other door and wait for Marissa to open it.

When Baptiste would have followed them, she held him back. "Give them a minute."

"How will we know if they're keeping their end of the deal?"

"Because they're strangely honest that way. It shouldn't be long," she murmured.

Whoop. Whoop.

A siren blared and Marissa murmured, "That's our cue."

They emerged to find a haze of smoke, making visibility difficult. People yelled. Leprechauns giggled. Things crashed and broke.

In that chaos, Marissa led him down a hall and through a door marked exit. The dumpsters rattled as they passed them. The alley lead to a parking lot that held many cars, but not Marissa's, which he knew for a fact remained at her house.

"Now what?" he asked.

A set of keys jangled as she held them up. "We're borrowing Ralph's wheels. Although, I will apologize in advance."

"For what?" he asked as he followed her quick stride to a rusted sedan.

"The mess." She unlocked the doors to the car and announced, "I'm driving." Good idea since she knew the city better than him.

The interior of the vehicle had food wrappers strewn and smelled heavily of deep-fried food, but he didn't care. He was out of the cell. Time to find Daphne.

Marissa started the car and didn't waste time getting them moving. As they exited the parking lot, a blacked-out SUV was pulling up in front of the building. He turned around to see who got out and growled, "There's my fucking uncle."

We really should eat his face.

Baptiste might make an exception to his "no eating people" rule, just for Frederick.

"We got out just in time, then. It won't be long before they notice us gone and how we left. We need to ditch this car," Marissa stated as she took a hard right.

"They took my truck keys, but I have a spare set in the wheel well."

"Can't take your truck or my car. They'll be looking for them."

"But I need wheels to get to Palusville."

"Obviously. Good thing I have a solution."

The pair of motorcycles she borrowed from a friend suited his growly mood.

We're coming, Daphne.

Hopefully, they wouldn't be too late.

CHAPTER 12

CIRCE LIVED. THE SHOCK OF IT ROOTED DAPHNE.

Mother, why didn't you tell me?

No answer. Then again, what could the Earth Mother say that would forgive this betrayal?

A seething Daphne faced the witch who'd trapped her for centuries. "I am going to kill you!" A threat without any power because the iron cuffs kept Daphne weak.

"Me? Shouldn't you be mad that your precious Mother would leave you stuck in that tree for so long? I mean, how hard is it to break a curse?" The witch tapped her chin and pretended to think. "Oh, that's right, very hard when it's tied to a ley line that's constantly feeding it." She cackled an ugly sound that didn't match her exterior.

While centuries old, Circe still appeared in her prime, her golden hair hinting only lightly of silver. Her face was mostly smooth but for a few lines by her eyes and forehead, her trim figure tall and straight.

"Thanks for the rest. I needed a break," Daphne lied.

"Oh, how lovely. Pretending you don't have a burning hatred for me." Again, Circe giggled nastily. "I'll admit I had a feeling when I felt my spell finally snap that you'd come for vengeance. I put out word that any dryads spotted in the area should be brought to me."

"You're the one who corrupted the Cryptid Authority."

"Didn't take much. Kidnap a few family members, kill a few to show I'm serious, and it's amazing how much they'll ignore in the hopes I won't eliminate the rest."

The prideful taunting had Daphne wishing for something sharp to jab in her ears so she wouldn't have to listen. The witch had no remorse, only arrogance. But she must also have a plan. What happened here wasn't by accident.

"You've been poisoning the land," Daphne stated.

Circe waved a hand. "An unfortunate side effect to my experiments."

"Experiments to do what?"

"Become a goddess, of course. I'm so close. I've managed to defy aging and sickness. Even regrew a hand after an incident." Circe held up the limb and twisted it to show off. "At this point, I've amassed so much magic the next logical step is divinity itself."

"You can't make yourself into a god," Daphne exclaimed.

"Why not?"

"Because gods aren't created."

"Then where do they come from?" Circe countered.

"Nowhere. They're divine. They just are." Daphne had never wondered before.

"Are they, though? Or are they simply beings who found a way to push their power to the next level?"

"Even if they were, what does that have to do with the people you've been murdering?"

"I need their souls." A mad light danced in Circe's gaze. "The idea occurred to me as I was torturing a hitchhiker. When he died, a burst of energy was expelled from his body, and it made me think of the gods and their quest to be worshipped. 'Why?' I asked myself. Why would they care if anyone believed in them unless it conveyed extra power? Only, what power? Humans have none. Belief is a feeling, not a tangible thing. The only thing a non-cryptid has is a soul. Their life force. What if, when they die, those souls go to the gods they worship? That led me to my experiments. It turns out, holding on to souls after death isn't easy. I've managed to contain them, but the side effect is..." Circe glanced around. "Somewhat detrimental to the environment. But that's only because I've yet to figure out how to harness their power for my own use."

"And to think they call *me* psycho," Daphne muttered.

Circe's face creased into an ugly rictus. "I'm not crazy. You'll see. Lately I've been expanding my collection to cryptids. And what better soul to capture than that of a champion? I can't wait to see what happens when I add your life essence to my collection."

"I will stop you," Daphne promised.

"Like you stopped me before?" The witch cackled.

"Maybe it's time you remembered what happened and why you should have never come after me again."

The witch waved her hands and suddenly Daphne wasn't outside the cottage with its polluted yard, but back in time before the roads and buildings, before women wore trousers and people bathed regularly.

She stood outside and observed a young dryad with silvery hair listening to the frightened townsfolk talking about a witch cursing their crops and poisoning their wells because they'd refused to pay a tithe. Daphne had been so cocky. Strutting about without a care. After all, the Mother chose her to be her champion. Someone to help those who couldn't help themselves.

Future Daphne trailed herself as she strode boldly for the witch's tower, a tall stone affair with a surprisingly lush garden outside. A garden fed by bodies, as it turned out. Their legs stuck out from the soil and acted as braces for the tomato plants.

The witch had been killing all those who trespassed. But her real crime was the poisoning of the village lands and water supply because they refused to give in to her blackmail. Outside the garden, fields lay fallow, trees lost their leaves, dead fish floated to the shore of the river.

The Mother didn't tolerate that kind of abuse.

At the base of the tower with no door, Daphne shouted, "Come out and face the Earth Mother's judgement."

A woman peered from the topmost window and smirked. "I've done no wrong."

"You've harmed the land of your neighbors."

"Did I?"

"I am not here to play games. Come down at once."

"Make me," came the taunted reply.

Daphne, the undefeated champion, eyed the tower and chose to climb, her rooting fingers digging into the mortar and stone.

The witch disappeared from sight, most likely in fear.

An assumption that cost Daphne.

The slick oil that poured down didn't hurt until the torch that fell from above ignited it.

A screaming Daphne, covered head to toe in flames, lost her grip, falling to the ground and rolling to extinguish the inferno. Gravely injured, she staggered from the witch's property, aiming for the forest, but not quite making it. The pain sent her to the ground, sobbing. The Mother reacted by causing the Earth to heave and buckle, a rift opening in the ground to swallow her whole —the quake rippling outwards and tumbling the witch's tower.

The Mother wrapped Daphne in a healing cocoon from which a tree sprouted. As it drank in sunshine, air, and water, it fed Daphne, soothing her injuries. In that dreamlike state, she watched the world above. The villagers came with their pitchforks to stab through the tower's rubble, finding no body.

Is she dead?

The Mother replied, *No.*

Indeed, the witch hadn't just survived, she was angry at losing her home and blamed Daphne.

One night, as the world slept, with the Mother absent, since she followed the sun, the witch came to stand in front of Daphne's little sapling. Hands laced in front of her, the witch named Circe spat, "Because of you, I must leave and start over."

Daphne's consciousness rustled the branches and leaves, the message being, *Flee wherever, I will find you.*

"Only if you survive!" The witch flung a fireball at the tree, but the Mother had protected it against fire and so it extinguished rather than burned.

Circe tried lightning next.

It failed to split the slender trunk.

Even hacking at the bole with a blade had no effect. The Mother had protected the tree from harm.

The boughs swayed in mockery at Circe's attempt. But the witch wasn't done.

Daphne had never seen the dark kind of magic she called upon next, a magic that didn't harm the tree. On the contrary, the witch cast a spell of life, a life fed by a ley line diverted to run directly through its roots.

At the time, Daphne hadn't understood why the witch chuckled and said, "Enjoy eternity."

But as time passed and Daphne's wounds healed, she realized she could not escape. Her seed remained tucked within the aging tree. A tree that went through the seasons, and years, more than was normal for its type. The ley line kept it alive even as nature took its course. Bugs infested. Dry rot settled within. The poor tree cried out in pain. But no one heard.

Not even the Mother. The ley line and the curse kept the Mother away.

And so Daphne waited...

...centuries.

Until the right people came along and broke the spell, releasing her into a world vastly changed.

Daphne woke from the memory, fearful for a moment that she'd lost yet more eons but the cage she found herself trapped in had a view of Circe's cottage. The bars were of iron and sizzled her palms when she gripped them. The floor was metal plated and burned her soles. She reached between the rods to try and touch the ground, wanting contact with the Mother, but the witch had sprinkled it with salt. Even if it weren't, in this poisoned place, Daphne doubted the Mother would have heard.

Would the Mother even care? After all, she'd let Circe live, then led Daphne to the witch who'd hurt her. Did the Mother want her to die?

She could have sworn she heard a faint whisper, *Have faith.*

Hard to have faith in such a situation.

A rumble in the distance drew her attention, a growl like the one she'd heard not long ago. The motorcycle came into view, holding a big man with an intent expression.

Her lips parted.

Baptiste.

The beast had come for her.

The elation within had her smiling in greeting, only to frown. He'd come alone and bore no weapon. Foolish. So much for being rescued.

He parked the motorcycle and slid off, his gaze focused on her. "You okay, Psycho?"

"Do I look okay? I'm in an iron cage," she grumbled.

He glanced at the cottage. "Is the witch inside?"

"I don't know where she is but you'd best hurry. She most likely knows you're here."

"I'm coming. Don't get your roots in a twist." He swaggered in her direction, looking nonchalant, but she saw the tension that had his eyes scanning the area, the way his nose twitched ever so slightly as he scented.

"This isn't the time for levity. The witch is Circe, my old enemy," she stated.

"So I've heard. Fucking CA handed you over." He passed the bubbling cauldron with a frown.

"They were trying to save the lives of their captured agents."

"At the expense of yours," he growled as his boot crunched some brittle bones on the ground.

She rolled her shoulders. "I'm better equipped to handle her."

"Says the woman in a cage."

"Did you come here just to insult me?" she groused.

"I'm here to save you-ooo!" He yelped as he suddenly got yanked off his feet by a hidden snare. The tether around his ankle had him dangling upside down and she couldn't help but laugh.

"Doing a great job with the rescue," she snickered.

He scowled. "A temporary setback." His shirt rode up his body, but he paid it no mind as he bent in half, using his abdominal muscles, which flexed admirably as he reached to grab the rope. It took him but a moment to release the loop from his ankle, then he dropped to the ground.

Despite doing it quickly, he ran out of time.

Circe appeared suddenly in a puff of smoke. "If it isn't the wood nymph's lover. Say goodnight." With a snap of her fingers, the witch put Baptiste to sleep, the spell buckling his knees and sending him to the ground in a heap.

So much for Daphne getting out of the cage.

"Leave him alone!" she futilely yelled.

"Or what?" Circe shifted to face her. "What will you do? Yell? Stomp your feet?"

The helplessness enraged Daphne. How was she supposed to fight the witch when she had all the advantages? "You won't get away with this."

"And yet I already have. I've defeated all those sent against me. None are a match for my power!" Circe boasted.

It took everything in Daphne to not react when Baptiste stood up behind Circe a finger to his lips.

He wasn't asleep!

Daphne had to keep the witch distracted.

"One day someone wilier than you is going to take you out."

"Not you," smirked Circe.

"No, not me," Daphne huffed. "But I will cheer when it happens."

"It won't, but even if it did, you won't be around—" The last of her words got cut off as Baptiste wrapped his big hands around Circe's neck and squeezed, lifting her from the ground.

Circe scratched at his hands, clawing as she gasped for air. Her eyes bulged. Her motions became frantic. The magic she tried to call fizzled as he choked her.

Crack.

Circe's neck snapped and she went limp.

The witch was dead. Daphne almost pouted since she'd been wanted to be the one who killed.

Baptiste dropped the body and approached the cage.

"Nice job faking sleep," she remarked as he grabbed the bars on her cage and gave them a yank.

"I'm just glad she didn't notice Marissa cast a repelling spell on me or things might have ended differently," he admitted.

"Marissa helped you." A flat reply at odds with the ire brewing within.

"Yeah. When we escaped the CA, she was the one to find us the bikes. We split up at the main road. She was supposed to meet us here as the plan was I'd approach from the front and she'd circle around and come in at the rear. I hope she didn't run into trouble." He glanced off into the distance with concern.

Daphne muttered, "I'm sure the pretty witch is fine."

His gaze returned to her with a lopsided smile. "Is she pretty? I hadn't noticed." He heaved on the bars, and with a grunt, they squealed and began to bend, just not enough for her to get out.

"Hold on, I can help." A huffing Marissa suddenly appeared, looking disheveled, with rotted leaves caught in her hair and some kind of putrid stain on her pants. She waved her hands and bit her lip as she aimed at the cage, grunting, "Someone didn't want you escaping. These bars are like iron metal on steroids."

"Let me see if there's a saw that can cut through or

something to pry them apart inside." He glanced at Daphne. "I'll be right back. Don't go anywhere."

She snorted. "Ha. So funny."

His lips quirked. "I try. I'll be quick." He headed for the cottage while Marissa kept straining only to finally grouse, "I can't get them loose. My magic isn't as strong here."

"The whole place is unnaturally tainted," Daphne stated.

"What was she doing?" Marissa eyed the cauldron and bones.

"Ungodly things." An ironic way of putting it.

An impatient Marissa planted her hands on her hips. "What is taking that man so long? Is he looking with his ass?"

Daphne snickered. It seemed some things hadn't changed since she'd been gone, including men being inept at finding items.

"While he's fucking around inside, I'm going to check the wood pile I saw around back. Maybe there's an axe."

Marissa didn't make any jokes as she sauntered off, leaving Daphne alone in the stupid cage. Foiled by metal. It was so unfair.

Movement drew her eye and dropped her jaw as Circe, her head at a decidedly unhealthy angle, rose from the ground.

"You're dead!" Daphne exclaimed.

"As if I'd be so easy to kill. I will heal from this. And when I do, I'll be back for you, *Champion*." With slash of her hand, smoke enveloped Circe and when it dissipated, the witch was gone.

Just in time for Baptiste to emerge with a jug. He held it up, crowing, "I found some acid that should melt those suckers." It took him a second to notice. "Where's the body?"

"Gone. Circe is still alive."

CHAPTER 13

Should have let me eat the witch.

For once, Garou had a point.

"I snapped her neck. How can she be alive?" Baptiste asked as he kicked at the bones on the ground.

"She's been dabbling in some dark magic." Daphne's lips twisted. "Really dark stuff, to the point the Mother can't penetrate it and Marissa stated she couldn't access her full power."

Bad place, Garou agreed.

"This place is all kinds of unhealthy. I recommend we get out of here ASAP before we start looking like those trees."

"Any time you're ready," she replied dryly.

"Stand back from the bars while I weaken them with this acid." He tried not to wonder why the witch had such potent stuff on hand as he knelt and poured the liquid in the jug around the welded joints. The fumes had Daphne covering her nose. He tried to be more masculine about it and let those nasal hairs burn.

As he began kicking the bars with his heavy boots, Marissa came around the cottage empty-handed. Not that it mattered. The bars snapped from the base and with a twisted yank, he managed to create a space large enough for the dryad to exit.

"Yay! You're free." Marissa clapped her hands.

"Now's not the time to celebrate," Daphne grumbled.

"What's wrong?" asked the pink-haired witch.

"Circe's still alive despite her snapped neck." Baptiste filled her in.

Marissa's mouth rounded. "How is that possible?"

"Because she's found a way to heal major injuries. Should have taken her head," Daphne huffed.

Decapitation tended to make death permanent.

"Sh-ee-it," Marissa drawled. "You think she's still close by?" She eyed the rotted trees around the cottage suspiciously.

"Most likely since this is a power hub for her. Which is why we need to take care of it," Daphne said grimly.

"How?" Baptiste queried.

"She's poisoned the land with her blood magic and sacrifices, but there's one thing that cleanses." Daphne moved to the cauldron and kicked it over, spilling its noxious contents on the ground. She then crouched by the fire pit with its glowing embers. She glanced at him over her shoulder. "We need to start a fire. A big one."

He whistled. "If we get one going, this whole forest will burn down and possibly part of the town."

"If we're going to weaken Circe and cut her off from her power, we have no choice. She's drawing strength from what she's done here. It has to be released."

Marissa bobbed her head. "She's right. I can feel the wrongness. It's sunk into everything around: trees, ground. It's even permeating the air."

"She had some bottles of cooking oil inside. We can soak some sheets with it and use them as wicks," Baptiste suggested.

In short order, they'd gathered as many flammable items as they could find, including bottles of alcohol. They created a trail that started from the motorcycle and branched out into the forest and the cottage.

Baptiste eyed their work with satisfaction. "This should get a decent blaze going."

"Your optimism is commendable considering the moist decay will resist our attempt to cleanse," Daphne muttered.

"Here's to hoping I make it to my bike before the flames," Marissa chirped. "At least this time I can use the driveway and not cut through the woods."

"You and Daphne should take the bike. I'm better equipped to run," he offered. "Just take my clothes with you so I don't end up riding naked once I get to the road."

"Now that would a sight to see." Marissa laughed.

"The fire won't move that quickly," Daphne huffed. "No one has to get naked."

She's jealous again! Garou exclaimed.

Marissa waggled her fingers. "Actually, while the offer is nice, I planned to stay behind so I can make sure the flames take proper hold."

"What if Circe is nearby?" Baptiste countered. "Or the fire spreads faster than expected?"

"I don't think she's around. As for the other, I can

shield myself from the worst of it and I am pretty fast on my feet. I used to run track."

Daphne nodded. "She's correct. Circe is no longer here. The ominous weight of this place lessened once she disappeared."

"Shoo!" Marissa waved them off. "Let's get this shithole burning before that changes. I'll meet you on the road."

"Ready?" he queried, seeing that Daphne appeared lost in thought.

She shook herself. "Yes."

Baptiste led the way to the motorcycle and straddled it, knowing his bulk left but a tiny sliver of seat at his back. Daphne pursed her lips at the sight.

"Get on." He grabbed the handles and the motor growled.

"There isn't much room," she noted.

"Not much I can do about that, Psycho, other than tell you to cuddle up close and hold on tight," he advised.

"I do not cuddle," she grumbled as she swung her leg over the bike. Her arms went around his wide middle, too wide for her hands to touch. It plastered her against his back. He enjoyed the closeness a little too much.

She fits just right.

Indeed, she did.

He put a hand over hers. "It's going to be noisy and windy. Whatever you do, don't let go."

"I'm not an idiot."

"I'm aware you're not. But this is going to be a new experience for you. Just giving you some warning."

Expecting a sassy retort, her "Thank you," took him by surprise.

We will protect her with our life, Garou promised.

Indeed. "I won't let anything happen to you." An admission he'd not meant to speak aloud and to hide his embarrassment, he twisted the throttle. The motorcycle barely lurched and yet she squeezed tight, making him chuckle.

"Now that's what I call a hug."

"Shut up and drive." Daphne rested her cheek against him, and he appreciated the trust as he had a feeling it wasn't something she offered often. The ride up the driveway to the road ended all too soon, with him rolling to a stop beside Marissa's vacant motorcycle.

When Daphne would have disembarked, he put a hand over hers, keeping her in place with her arms around him. "Stay on the bike in case we need to make a fast getaway." Not the entire reason. He just liked having her close.

Together on the bike, they watched the forest hiding Circe's cottage. At first, there was nothing to be seen. Then a curl of smoke appeared, quickly thickening above the canopy. The trees began to shiver.

"I wonder what's making the trees move like that? Is it magic?" he mulled aloud.

"It's because they're reacting to the fire," she murmured softly. "They are crying out."

"Fuck me. I didn't even think..." he stammered. "The fire... The trees... Are you okay with this?" How traumatizing this must be for her, given her dryad nature.

"I'll be fine. It's just difficult to hear. Despite these

not being the sentient variety they are aware. For too long they've been suffering because of Circe's actions. Now they are thankful that they are finally being given relief."

"If you say so." He wasn't convinced.

"While some see fire as the ultimate destruction—and in some ways it is—it also paves the way for renewal and rebirth. The trees that die today will provide the nutrient-dense ash from which their seedlings will rise, reclaiming this land."

The explanation eased his mind somewhat until he noticed another oddity: The lack of fleeing forest animals. Not a single squirrel emerged. No mice scurried. Even the sky remained empty of birds. It made him wonder how long it took Circe to destroy this area.

Centuries. And me too busy to notice, the Mother replied in his mind, startling him and Garou, who snapped, *Keep your paws off my avatar.*

"Um, your goddess just spoke to me."

"I heard," Daphne stated, irritation in her voice. "The Mother has much to answer for, starting with her not telling me Circe lived."

Because I feared you'd be foolish in your pursuit if you knew the witch had found a way to extend her natural lifespan.

Again, the voice spoke, making Garou howl loud enough in his head that Baptiste almost missed Daphne's reply.

"Instead of being forewarned, I fell into a trap. A trap you had me walk straight into," Daphne accused. "You told me not to fight, to go along with my kidnapping."

Some things must happen a certain way for other things to follow. The non-answer from the Mother had Daphne growling.

Baptiste understood her irritation and offered a commiserating, "Gods are annoying."

"Agreed."

Hey! Garou took offense.

A crackling noise drew their attention to a section of forest where the glow of flames made an appearance.

"Come on, Marissa, where are you?" he muttered. He might have just met her, but the witch seemed like the good sort who didn't deserve to be toasted alive.

"You're awfully concerned about her," Daphne remarked sourly.

"She's been a good ally who doesn't deserve harm for helping me find you."

"Only an ally?"

He patted her hand. "No need to be jealous." He tested Garou's theory.

"I am not jealous!" she huffed. "If you're so worried about her, why don't you go rescue her?"

"I am not leaving you alone."

"I can take care of myself."

"You can. But that doesn't mean you should have to."

Just then, movement on the driveway turned into a running Marissa, her long hair streaming behind as she sprinted.

"That shit is burning better than expected," the witch exclaimed as she neared.

"The trees might be moist with rot on the outside,

but within they were dried husks, and they wanted to burn," Daphne solemnly stated.

Marissa stopped by her bike to look back at the inferno billowing smoke. "It's burning all right. We should get out of here. I am getting this weird pressure-like feeling, as if something is about to blow."

As if her words brought it to reality, an explosion caused the ground to rumble. A moment later, a shockwave rolled through them, knocking Marissa to her ass. Her bike hit the ground. Baptiste only barely kept his upright in the concussion, his hand once more over Daphne's, holding her against him.

By the time the wave of force subsided, a good portion of the forest had toppled, and the fire burned harder than before.

A groaning Marissa picked herself up off the ground and brushed herself off. "I think whatever reservoir of power Circe built just released."

The souls are now at peace, the Mother declared.

Marissa blinked. "Um, did anyone else hear that?"

Her expression led to Daphne snickering. "The Mother blesses you with her wisdom."

"Don't let Hekate hear that. She wouldn't be happy if she thought your goddess was trying to poach." Marissa grinned. "As if I'd ever change sides."

Marissa used magic to stand her bike back up, and after she straddled it Baptiste asked, "Where to?"

"I'm going to head home right after I gas this baby and make a few calls to report the malfeasance in my office," Marissa declared. "Once the coast is clear, I'll give you a shout so you can come grab your truck. In the meantime, I'd recommend you hole up in a motel out of sight."

"I need to find Circe," a stubborn dryad stated.

"Obviously we need to find her. But given we just destroyed her base of power, I think we can hold off a day or two while I get shit cleared up and call in some reinforcements to help. It will be a lot easier if we have the CA working with us instead of against."

"You think you can have those who worked with Circe removed that quickly?" Baptiste questioned.

"Seeing as how I was already working with somebody in Cryptid Special Investigations, I'm hoping we can move quickly. Our biggest problem is lack of concrete proof. I don't know if just Daphne's testimony will be enough so here's to hoping I can dig up a paper trail or finagle some phone logs showing a connection to get the ball rolling. Meaning I need you to hang tight for at least a day before you go off witch hunting. Can you do that?" Marissa aimed the last at Daphne.

"Fine." A begrudging agreement from the dryad.

Marissa waved as she gunned her motorcycle and headed out.

Baptiste glanced best he could over his shoulder. "Any preferences as to where we go?"

"I don't suppose any of these hotels have a nice garden? That forest left a taint."

"Actually, I saw just the place on the way in. Think you can hold on for thirty minutes or so?"

She clung tight to him as he returned to a sign he'd seen when he'd been racing to find Daphne. *Cabins for rent.*

Rustic, small, but surrounded by nature.

As for the fact they had only one bed?

Perfect. Garou approved.

Baptiste, however, would be fine sleeping on the floor so long as it kept him close to Daphne.

If he'd realized one thing when he'd been flying down the highway on his way to rescue her, it was that he might not have known the dryad long, but he felt something for her.

More than annoyance.

More than attraction.

Garou said it best. *Mine.*

The problem being, he had no idea how she felt about him.

The cabin he rented was the one furthest from the rest. Bathed in a late afternoon sun that filtered through healthy green trees, the A-frame didn't have much room inside, not that Daphne cared.

She sat outside, lotus style on the picnic table. Eyes closed. Hands on her knees. Face uplifted to the sun. She looked peaceful.

Beautiful.

As she communed with nature, he kept watch from the porch. Guarding. Admiring. But nothing more.

He'd almost forgotten why he didn't deserve pleasure.

He most certainly wasn't worthy of someone like Daphne.

But that didn't stop the yearning.

CHAPTER 14

DAPHNE FELT THE BEAST'S GAZE ON HER. ANYONE ELSE SHE might have snapped and told them to look elsewhere or lose their eyes. But with Baptiste, she found a certain measure of satisfaction in knowing he watched.

Someone coyer might have simply assumed he did it to safeguard her meditation, however, the tingling awareness in her body claimed otherwise. Add in his previous smoldering interest and the protectiveness, all signs that indicated he cared for her as more than simply a companion on a quest.

He wants me.

At the same time, she knew he'd never actually do anything about it. He remained too busy flagellating himself.

She, on the other hand, saw no reason to abstain. On the contrary, she found herself thinking of him, wondering what it would be like to take him as a lover.

The man had come to her rescue. A novelty. Daphne had never had anyone save her intentionally before.

Usually, Daphne had to be the hero, the one risking her life for others. It felt nice to have someone who cared enough to put themselves in peril for her.

As the sun set, he approached and draped a blanket around her shoulders. The simple and kind gesture drew her gaze to him.

"Hungry?" he asked.

In that moment she realized she was, but not for food.

Daphne had never learned the art of flirting. She didn't know how to be subtle, hence why she launched herself at his body and mashed her mouth to his. A kiss that lacked finesse and caught him by surprise.

He recovered quickly, his hesitancy lasting only a second before he returned her embrace. His hands drew her against his solid frame. He hummed as he kissed her, a low, growling sound that sent shivers throughout her body.

Being Baptiste, he pulled away. "We shouldn't."

"Why not?" she complained.

"Because."

The one word arched her brow. "That's not a reason."

His lips flattened. "Because I'm not worthy."

At that reply, she snorted. "According to you."

"How about because a day ago you barely tolerated me."

"If I didn't tolerate you, I would have never asked you to come with me on my quest."

"Is this your way of saying you like me?"

"Do you think I'd be kissing you if I didn't?" She arched a brow. Then because he didn't look convinced, she added, "I like how you look." Rugged and strong. "I like how you feel." She stroked a hand down the front of his solid chest. "I like how you are brave and didn't abandon me even if it would have been simpler."

He frowned. "I wasn't about to let you come to harm if I could prevent it."

"And for that alone, you are worthy," she murmured, drawing close for a soft, tender kiss.

When she tugged at his shirt, he murmured, "Shall we go inside for some privacy?"

"No. I like it out here." At one with nature.

His lips quirked. "Good thing the next cabin over is empty then or we might have management coming over to complain."

"Complain about people doing what is natural?"

"Natural for you and me, but the humans tend to be more prudish about public displays of affection."

Her lips quirked. "Then they should look away."

At her response, he chuckled. "You really are unique."

"And impatient. Take off your shirt," she demanded.

"As you command." He stripped the garment, leaving his chest bare for her to skim her hands over. She touched him, reveling in the texture of his flesh, teasing the hair on his chest that arrowed down to the waist of his pants. She slid the top button from its loop.

"Not so quick." He put his hands on hers.

"Why?"

"Maybe we should take things slow."

"I don't have the patience for that." To prove her point, she removed her own shirt, leaving her bare as she wore no brassiere. She'd refused when Nelly showed her the confining contraption.

His eyes glowed as he beheld her bared breasts. "Like perfect peaches," he murmured.

She shifted from her meditative pose to kneel on the picnic table, the only way to properly kiss him given their height difference. She laced her arms around his neck as she pressed her nipples to his chest, enjoying the friction that puckered them.

It had been a long time since she'd desired, but despite that she recognized there was something electric about his touch. Something meltingly pleasurable in his kiss.

His hands cupped her buttocks, squeezing and pulling her against him, his confined erection still very much noticeable against her lower belly even with their trousers in the way. The fabric impeded her need to be close to him. Skin to skin.

She stood suddenly so that she might tug at her pants, pulling them down over her legs, baring herself to him. Before she could kneel again, he nuzzled her mound. Heat shot through her. A weakness of limbs too. She clutched his hair to steady herself as her legs threatened to buckle.

But she didn't fall. He held her effortlessly and did nothing more than rest his face against her pubes. She wanted more than cuddles though.

She gripped his head and pushed it to where she wanted it. Between her legs.

He growled. "Let's get you in a better position if I'm going to feast."

By that he meant lying her down on the table, her legs spread and him bent over between them.

He blew hotly on her, his breath making her shiver and gasp. The first lick had her arching and digging her fingers into the wood. He tasted her, his tongue spreading her nether lips to taste her nectar. His lips slid and teased, gripping her clitoris, making her pant and keen as pleasure flowed through her, awakening desires long dormant. Like a tree after a long winter, she came to life, her juices flowing and being tapped by the man determined to make her orgasm.

He flicked his tongue fast against her, making her whimper as her body tightened. When her climax hit, her whole body bowed, rising in an arch as a wave of bliss took her and kept rocking her.

When it subsided, she remained tingly, aware of everything, and not ready to stop. She sat up on the table and reached for him, kissing the lips sticky with her sap. Her hands tugged at his pants to release his erection, hard and thick, a bough that wouldn't break.

Her legs went around his hips as she guided, pulling him into her still-quivering channel, locking him into place. She sucked on his lower lip as he groaned. His fingers dug into her buttocks while his whole body trembled.

She wiggled until she was off the table and supported by him, an angle that pushed him deeper. Holding her, he bounced her up and down, the short slams jolting a pleasurable spot inside that soon had her panting and her body tightening again.

Faster.

Deeper.

Harder.

Their breathing emerged raggedly as they found a rhythm that had her coiling before climaxing again. Her orgasm squeezed him tight and drew a harsh cry from him as he spilled his seed hotly inside her.

He rested his forehead against hers as their bodies calmed and cooled, the night air wicking the sweat.

"Wow," he finally rumbled.

"That was better than expected," she agreed.

He shook his head and his reply held amusement. "Glad to know I didn't disappoint."

She doubted he ever would. There was something about him that drew her like no other.

"About that food you were mentioning..." she said rather than spew something completely sappy and unlike her.

"Does my psycho need sustenance?"

"She does if we're going to be doing that again before bed."

He stilled before tilting her chin for a kiss. "In that case, I'd better go grab us some food and whipped cream for dessert." A comment she didn't understand until he licked it from her body later that night.

A body that came so hard, she thought she'd died of pleasure.

As they snuggled in bed afterwards, he held her close to him, the steady thud of his heartbeat soothing.

When she woke before him, she found herself still desirous, and it took but a few strokes of her hands on his flesh before he pulled her atop him, and she rode him to a glorious sunrise.

While she lay sated and her muscles lazy, he dressed, giving her a soft smile as he said, "There's a breakfast place across the road from the main rental office. I'll go grab us something to fill our bellies. Try to not get in any trouble or kill anyone while I'm gone."

Her lips curved. "Worried I'll have fun without you?"

At that, he laughed. "Yes. I won't be gone long."

Only he didn't return and as she dressed, she suddenly paused as a wave of emotion hit her. Anger. Not hers, but the beast's. Then worry. Not for himself, but her.

Perturbed, she went to stand outside, wondering if she should seek him out when the Mother whispered, *It's too late. He's been taken.*

And Daphne would wager she knew by whom.

CHAPTER 15

Despite leaving a warm bed with a sexy, naked dryad, Baptiste found himself whistling as he walked across the resort property and headed for the greasy spoon across the road.

Last night had been unexpected in a good way.

Best day ever! Garou chimed in.

It had been. Daphne's sudden seduction, while surprising, had allowed him to finally accept something Garou had been saying all along.

One, he didn't have to forever punish himself. Yes, he could feel guilty about what happened, but that didn't mean he could never be happy. And secondly...

She was meant for us.

Having been with his fair share of women, Baptiste could safely say he'd never experienced the mind-blowing, out-of-body pleasure he'd found with Daphne. She fulfilled him in the way he'd heard of but never expected. At first, she'd come across as abrasive, but he'd come to appreciate her forthright nature. There was no bullshitting in her world. She told it as it was. She didn't tolerate idiocy, nor did she hold back. It made her choice of taking him as her lover all the more special.

Even better, she made him feel happy. Hopeful. Excited about the future.

Blah. Blah. Stop being so sappy and move faster. That witch is still out there somewhere.

A reminder that hastened his steps across the street. How long would it take Circe to heal from a broken neck? A month? A week? A day? Last time he broke a leg, it took him seventy-two hours from getting the fracture to nothing showing on his x-ray. Would she heal that quickly?

He hoped not. At least they'd destroyed her base of power. Circe now would only be able to draw on her innate power and not the pool she'd been accumulating. Still, there was cause for concern as Circe's sadism made her wily. Baptiste might be tough, but not invulnerable. It would take just a well-timed lightning strike that would temporarily fry his nerves, or a sleep spell while he was unprotected for his ass to get taken out, leaving Daphne vulnerable. Marissa had made a good point that they could use help. But who could they trust if the CA had been compromised?

Having reached the diner, Baptiste ordered some pastries, hashbrowns, and breakfast sandwiches—minus meat for him—along with some freshly squeezed juice. While he waited, he sat on a stool, staring out the big window overlooking the main road. While it was still early, the restaurant had more than a few patrons. A prickling at his nape had him turning to scan the folks inside. No one appeared to be looking in his direction. Must be his paranoia.

No, I sensed someone watching too. Beware, Garou cautioned.

"Here's your order," stated the woman working the cash register.

Baptiste gathered the bag of food in one hand, tray of drinks in the other. As he exited, he eyed the cars parked. No dark-tinted SUVs like his uncle employed.

He waited for traffic to pass before starting to cross the road, noticing a sedan sitting at the exit for the resort. At his back in the diner's parking lot, he heard the sudden start and purr of an engine as someone prepared to leave. His stride quickened to get out of the way.

He didn't move fast enough.

A vehicle slammed into him from behind, scooping him onto the hood. The drinks flew, and the paper bag ripped. As Baptiste rolled off the hood, he had to hold on to Garou lest he shift in front of an audience. The world might know about werewolves, but the Garou? He was usually kept under wraps.

Danger!

No shit. Baptiste hit the pavement on his feet but hunched over as he tried to recover. He didn't feel the pain yet. That would come later when the bruising blossomed.

He heard more than saw the driver's side door of the car that hit him open. He lifted his head, ready to give the person shit, only to pause.

"Jules?" He recognized the man, part of his Pack.

"Don't make this hard," Jules said, holding up the dreaded tranq gun.

"How about you walk away?" Baptiste countered.

"You know I can't do that," Jules replied, his gaze flicking to something over Baptiste's shoulder.

Run, you idiot.

Before Baptiste could whirl to flee, the dreaded silver net came down over him.

Not again!

"No!" he roared, pulling at the burning silver strands. Before he could even start removing it, a lasso landed over him and tightened, pulling his arms to his side. "Release me." A growl that went unheeded. His laser-like glare didn't do anything to deter his uncle who strutted across the road, having emerged from the car waiting by the resort exit.

"Hello, nephew." Uncle Frederick wore a suit and sunglasses that did little to hide his emotionless face.

"Don't you fucking hello me. Tell your goons to untie me."

"I think not."

"How did you find me?"

"As if I wouldn't be watching your credit cards," Frederick chided.

"What do you want?" Baptiste snarled, angry at his own stupidity. Blame his distraction with Daphne. The woman had him all twisted up and not thinking straight.

"You know what I want. The Garou to lead the Pack as he was meant to."

"How many times do I have to tell you, I'm not interested."

Speak for yourself. I'm meant for greatness.

His uncle shook his head. "I'm aware of your lack of goals, and that's unfortunate as it means I'll have to resort to drastic measures."

"You mean like assaulting and kidnapping?" was his sarcastic reply.

"We both know neither of those will be enough to convince you to take your place as leader of the Packs."

"Then what? Going to lock me up until I agree?"

No more cages! Garou bristled at the very suggestion.

"You're too stubborn for that." His uncle shook his head. "It's a shame really. I had such high hopes for you when you were a child. But then you started rebelling."

"By rebelling, you mean getting a job that wasn't Pack-approved?"

"The Pack had positions you could have filled that would have been better suited for an Alpha in training."

"Ever think I wanted to earn my position and not have it handed to me?" Baptiste had issues with how the Packs were run. It shouldn't be about being the strongest. Why not someone who cared and wanted the Pack to thrive instead?

"Your ideals have no place in the Pack." His uncle's reply was cold. "Which is why you've left me no choice. Jules, Plato, load him up and quickly. We're drawing unnecessary attention."

Hands covered in thick leather gloves gripped his arms and tugged him to the rear of the vehicle.

Baptiste didn't go willingly.

Don't let them take us alive!

A little drastic even for Garou, who howled in his

mind as they got tossed in the trunk. His uncle stood over the opening, blocking the rising sun. "I am sorry it came to this, nephew. But you left me no choice."

"Where are you taking me?"

"The compound of course."

To which Baptiste replied, "You know I'll just escape the first chance I get."

"I'm well aware, which is why I'm done giving you chances. The Pack needs the Garou."

"Too bad. He's not yours to have."

"Not yet. But he will be. Once you die, he'll be free to choose another."

Die? "You're going to kill me?" He couldn't stem his incredulity.

"It's the only way."

"And how does that help you control the Garou? What if the next scion the Garou chooses resides in another Pack?"

"Birth isn't the only way for the Garou to be reborn."

"What's the supposed to mean?" Because for once, Garou remained silent.

"You'll soon see, and most likely regret, but by then it will be too late." With that ominous announcement, the trunk shut, leaving him in the dark with his thoughts and an angry Garou.

Does he really think when I reincarnate, I will help him?

How about we worry about the fact he's planning to kill me? Baptiste snapped to his other side.

Not ideal, I'll admit. You've been a rather interesting host. Not to mention it took me decades to choose you.

Then help me stop him.

Maybe if you'd let me eat his face like I asked we wouldn't be in this spot. Now, as you humans like to say, we're fucked.

An ominous reply. Would this be how his life ended? How unfair. Especially after such an epic night.

And what of Daphne? What would she think when he didn't return? What would happen to her? What if Circe found her?

He had to escape.

Hours later, bound to a fat tree with ropes weaved in silver, in the midst of the well-guarded compound, he'd yet to find a way to do so.

Was nice knowing you. Garou thought their fate a foregone conclusion.

However, Baptiste wasn't ready to give up, not when he heard the Earth Mother whisper, *All things happen for a reason. Have faith. Help is coming.*

Which could only mean Daphne. Daphne against a Pack about to shift with the full moon.

They'd tear her apart.

And there wasn't a fucking thing he could do to stop it.

Awoooo!

CHAPTER 16

"Where is he?" Daphne asked the Mother because suspecting who had Baptiste and locating him were two different things.

His uncle has him inside the Pack compound. Heavily secured. You won't get in without help.

Help? Daphne would usually eschew any but the last time she got cocky, she was severely injured and cursed for centuries. Add in that Baptiste's life might very well end up in the balance and she truly couldn't take any chances.

Luckily, Baptiste had left his phone behind—which was password locked.

She glared at the device. "Open."

It didn't obey.

"I command you to give me access."

Also didn't work.

She glared at the annoying object, and as if it sensed her ire, it suddenly rang. The screen displayed a red and green circle.

Green meant go, so she poked it.

"Hi Baptiste," Marissa greeted.

"It's Daphne," she quickly corrected. "Baptiste has been taken."

A pause on the other end before Marissa replied, "Did Circe get him?"

"Worse than that. His uncle did. Mother says I should seek reinforcements to fetch him."

"Wait, the Pack has him?"

"Yes."

"Then I doubt he's in danger. He's one of them. Most likely he's annoyed, though. He doesn't seem to like his uncle much."

"They mean to harm him."

"What makes you say that?"

Daphne wasn't one to lie. "I can feel it."

To her surprise, Marissa didn't argue. "Do you know where he's being held?"

"Mother says they have him in their compound, under guard."

"Unfortunately, the CA doesn't have legal authority to enter," Marissa mused aloud.

"But they committed a crime. They kidnapped him."

"Doesn't matter. The Packs have their own laws. They police their own."

Excuses. Daphne didn't have the time or patience to hear them. "I don't care. I'm going after him."

"Of course. I'm sure we can figure something out once we get there. Where are you? I'll come get you."

"Wait, you're going to help? But you just said it was dangerous and you had no jurisdiction."

"And? If he needs rescuing, then I'm in. Where are you?"

"I'm in a cabin in the woods."

The correct reply but Marissa laughed. "You'll have to be more specific. I need an address."

A complicated thing to request from someone who'd yet to learn to read. In the end, Daphne had to go to the building where Baptiste had secured their use of the cabin and ask the person behind the counter to tell Marissa her location.

It felt like forever, waiting for her to arrive. Especially given Daphne's hunger. The sun tickling her skin was well and good, but the hard soil didn't allow her to dig in her toes and get any nourishment.

By the time Marissa pulled into the parking lot, Daphne was ready to chew the leaves from some trees. Luckily, she didn't have to harm any possibly distant relatives as the CA agent brought a cooling bag filled with beverages and snacks.

The cheese and crackers tided Daphne over until they hit something called McDonald's. The French fries—salty sticks of goodness—were the best thing she'd ever eaten.

Marissa helped unlock the phone with a waggle of her fingers, and as they made the long drive back to Nexus, Daphne called Nelly who answered, "Baptiste? Where are you? Your uncle has been calling the office multiple times a day, flipping out since you left town."

"Baptiste is gone. His uncle found him," Daphne stated. "He kidnapped Baptiste earlier this morning."

"Daphne?" Nelly didn't hide her surprise.

"Yes, it's me. I have his phone and am on my way back to Nexus to rescue him."

A pause. "If his uncle has him then he's in Pack territory. You won't be allowed inside."

"I wasn't going to ask permission."

Nelly coughed. Must have caught Clive's cold. "You'll have to wait until tomorrow."

"Why?"

"Full moon tonight. If you illegally enter Pack lands while they're in their moon phase, they will tear you apart."

"This can't wait."

Marissa interjected, "Your friend is right. You don't want to mess with wolves on a full moon."

"Baptiste doesn't have until tomorrow." Daphne couldn't have said why she stated it with such certainty.

"Is he being threatened?" Nelly asked.

"Yes. He needs to be rescued before the moon rises or we'll be conducting a mission of vengeance for his death."

"They won't kill him. He's the Garou," Nelly exclaimed.

"That is precisely why he's going to die," Daphne countered.

"Let me talk to Clive and see what we can arrange," Nelly stated before giving Marissa her address and then hanging up.

Marissa took her eyes off the road to glance at Daphne. "What makes you so sure he's in dire peril? Did your goddess warn you?"

For a moment, Daphne didn't know how to explain it. "Baptiste and I were intimate last night, and it appears to have left a type of bond between us." She frowned. "I can sense some of his emotions. He is angry. Also a bit afraid. He's in danger. And I keep getting the impression of the moon and blood."

A moment passed before Marissa said softly, "It would seem you've mated with the wolf."

"Yes, we had sex," Daphne repeated since Marissa apparently didn't grasp that simple concept the first time.

"Mated, as in bonded at a deeper level. It's why you can feel things about him."

"But he didn't bite me." Daphne knew about shifter claiming, and Baptiste had done many things—licked, sucked, nibbled, penetrated—but not once did he chomp down on her skin.

"Don't quote me, but I think the bite mark is more symbolic than anything. I believe a couple that is fated-to-be simply needs an intense moment, like sex, to forge the bond."

"Oh." For once Daphne had nothing to say.

"Are you okay with that?" Marissa carefully asked.

To which she retorted, "Jealous he's mine?"

"Uh, no. He's not my type, not to mention he only has eyes for you."

"He'd better or I will pluck them like grapes."

A vehement reply that led to Marissa chuckling. "Oh boy, you really do have the hots for him, and I get the sense the feeling is mutual. You should have seen how frantic he was when he was in that cell at the CA office. He only wanted to escape so he could go to your rescue."

"And now you see why I have to do the same. No matter the danger," Daphne swore.

"I get it. We'll find a way."

The promise and use of *we* had Daphne frowning. "Why are you helping me?"

"Because while we might have only recently met, I like you." Marissa grinned in her direction. "Not to mention, we've shared a home-cooked breakfast. That makes us friends."

"You do make excellent bacon."

"Can't believe your mate doesn't eat any. A non-carnivore wolf. It's not right," Marissa muttered, shaking her head.

"It makes him unique," Daphne agreed. Part of why she liked him.

Entering Nexus, Daphne felt the difference, a slight shiver that had Marissa remarking, "What the fuck was that?"

"We've entered the Monster King's domain," she murmured.

"Have you met him?" Marissa inquired.

"No. But Mother claims so long as I don't harm his subjects, he won't bother me."

"What about if his subjects are trying to kill you?"

"Self-defense is allowed. Just not active hunting. Mother claims it should not be an issue in his territory. The monsters know better than to disobey their king."

"Wild fucking shit," Marissa muttered. "An actual god living in a town."

"Where does your goddess reside?"

"No idea. She just talks to me at random. We've never met. What about you and the Earth Mother?"

"She is the ground we walk upon. She is in every living plant."

"Have you always been her champion?" Marissa asked as she paused at a stop sign and checked the screen with all kinds of lines that she called a map.

"No. I began as a simple dryad, gentle like my sisters of the grove. We danced. We weaved crowns of flowers. We ate the nectar of fruit and lay in the soft grasses with human men for pleasure. We lived carefree and happy."

"This doesn't sound like a story that ends well."

"Because it doesn't." Daphne's jaw stiffened. The tragedy might have happened centuries ago, but it remained vivid in her mind. "One day, while we were harvesting some honey from a nearby hive, the trees in our grove were cut down. A senseless act since their wood wasn't the type good for building. The humans did it to trap us so we wouldn't have a place to hide." Daphne paused. "They had nets woven with iron and they threw them over my sisters and took them captive."

"And you?"

"I hadn't returned with them. I'd stopped to play in the river. By the time I made my way to the grove, the torture had begun. I heard their screams as my sisters were violated and mutilated."

"Why didn't your goddess save them?"

"The Mother isn't one to act directly, and at night, she flees for the lands where the sun shines. There was no one to hear their cries but me."

"What did you do?"

Daphne bowed her head. "I took the axe lying by the stump of my tree, and when the men fell asleep, I began chopping." The blood had quickly rendered her grip slick and yet she'd kept swinging, the lifeless eyes of her sisters fueling her. The moans of those who'd survived giving her strength.

"How many did you kill?"

"There were six men. I killed three before the others woke." They'd converged on her, angry and taunting her with the things they'd do once they managed to capture her. "I expected to die. Wanted to because of my grief. Instead, I discovered what I was capable of. The vinelike extension of my arm that I used to pluck fruit gave me the reach to strangle the closest attacker. My skin turned hard as bark, my body dense as the bole of my trunk, making their blows ineffectual. My fingers rooted around the haft of the axe, making sure I didn't lose my grip."

"You found your inner strength," Marissa softly commented.

"I did, and in the morning, when the dawn bathed the bloody grove, the Mother returned and wept at what they'd done. The sisters who survived were inconsolable and so Mother took them into her bosom. But to me, she said, 'You are the bough who did not break despite the storm. You are the stave against those who did evil. And for your bravery, I name thee the Earth's Paladin, my champion.'"

"Wow. That's intense. Do you like being a paladin?"

"Yes. There is satisfaction to be found in meting out justice for those who cannot achieve it on their own."

"You're basically a CA agent," Marissa summarized.

"You work to protect humans. My task is guarding the Earth." But then because that sounded harsh, Daphne added, "We are both important when it comes to providing safety to all."

"We are. We're here."

Marissa parked in front of the building Nelly and Clive called home. Not the house where she'd first met them. Apparently, they'd borrowed that home. This was a much larger building that had several floors and what they called apartments specifically for CA agent use. Mostly empty since the Monster King came into power. As Nelly had stated, "Not much use for a Special Monster Unit when they've now got a big boss who makes sure they claw and paw the line."

Daphne remembered how to reach Nelly's door which opened before she could knock. "You made good time," Nelly remarked, "But we'll still be cutting it close to moon rise."

"Hey." Clive lifted his head from the computer he stared at for a moment. Daphne didn't quite understand the strange contraption. Yet. She planned to learn.

"I have returned," Daphne announced. "Do you have a plan for us to access this compound where Baptiste is being held?"

Clive pointed to his screen. "I think I've found a weak spot where we can get in unnoticed."

With that opening statement, they put their heads together to plan. Quickly, though. Time was running out, the moon would rise soon, and to make matters worse, once the sun set, the Mother and her extra help would be gone.

But that wouldn't stop Daphne from saving her beast.

I'm coming for you. And woe to any who stood in her way.

CHAPTER 17

THIS DISRESPECT WON'T GO UNPUNISHED. I WILL AVENGE YOU, my short-lived avatar.

Garou seemed to think Baptiste's death a foregone conclusion, making it hard for him to keep any kind of hope. He'd spent hours lashed to the tree and while a few Pack members noticed, their loyalty—and fear—of his uncle meant they did nothing to free him. Attempts to talk sense into them failed. As did threats. Difficult to seem imposing when their supposed god couldn't free himself.

I'm a wolf, not a wizard, grumbled Garou. *I promise, if given a chance, they will pay. I will tear out their innards and slurp them like noodles.*

While Baptiste appreciated the sentiment, he didn't want people he'd known his whole life to be massacred just because they'd chosen to listen to the wrong man. His misguided uncle was to blame for this.

If you'd accepted the role they offered... Garou's said slyly.

He'd have been trapped in a position he never wanted.

Uh-oh. Garou muttered.

"Now what?" he said aloud. Let the Pack hear him talking to Garou. If they thought him nuts, maybe they'd think twice about their actions.

Our favorite dryad is in Nexus.

Daphne had returned? How and why? Had she followed Circe here?

She's here for us, dummy.

"How can you be so sure?"

Can't you feel it?

"No."

Because you're back to stewing in self-pity. Pay attention.

He almost grumbled in reply, but instead took a steadying breath, then another, calming himself enough that he received a faint glimmer of emotions—anger and worry... about him. How was it he could feel Daphne's concern for him?

His eyes shot open as the reason why hit him. "We're mated!"

Ding. Ding. Ding. Give the dog a bone.

It must have been when they had sex, but... "I didn't bite her."

The biting is for appearance and to warn off other wolves. The true connection is at a whole different level.

"Wait a second, if I can sense her does that mean..."

She knows what you're feeling. Or should I say despairing? Yet in spite of your self-pity, she's determined to rescue you, which is really wolf-asculating by the way.

"She can't come here!" Baptiste strained at the silver

binding him, the burn of it barely noticeable in his newfound determination. "The whole Pack is about to converge on this clearing and the moon will rise soon." They'd kill any intruder.

Too late.

"No, it's not. Not so long as I am breathing. I have to get free," he growled.

You mean you haven't been trying this entire time?

"Save the sarcasm and try being useful for once."

Even if I could transform while bound in silver, you can't expect me to eat my subjects.

"What happened to slurping their intestines?"

I was trying to make you feel better.

"Those so-called subjects want to kill me, the body you're inhabiting, and while it's great you can resurrect in someone else, I won't."

It's a good thing I like you, Garou grumbled. *You're insolent and not at all reverent about the honor I bestowed upon you.*

"It's not an honor if it only brings me grief," he growled. "Tell me, exactly how has having you inside me improved my life?"

You're never alone.

"Not a selling point."

Because of me, you are bigger and stronger than everyone else.

"And? Have you seen how much my groceries cost to keep that body fueled?"

You know, most avatars are appreciative of having a piece of their god inhabiting their flesh, and they strive for greatness.

"You mean they go on a power trip that ends up in them being challenged and killed because they've become megalomaniacs." The last Garou manifestation had led to Packs warring because two avatars rose during the same time period, leading to a split that pitted them against each other.

An unfortunate mistake in my resurrection. That's the problem when your pieces are scattered. Although, you should feel honored that you have more of me than the previous scions.

"That honor is going to cost me my life," he grumbled.

A distant shout turned his head. It wasn't repeated and distraction arrived in the form of some Pack members gathering in the clearing before the massive oak tree. They were dressed in loose clothes and robes that would be easily shed before the moon rose and forced them to shift. Hooks were hammered into the trees at random, giving them a place to hang their garments so that they didn't get soaked by the dew. It didn't stop them from being chilly the next morning when pulled onto skin still warm from running in fur.

More than a few of the Pack stared openly at Baptiste. Some appeared disturbed and looked away. Others showed a strange excitement, the impending full moon shift rousing their bloodlust. Not one lifted a finger to help him.

It led to him growling in a voice deeper than usual, "Be it known that your scents have been marked. Your actions noted. Your betrayal will not be forgiven." Garou spoke through him, and Baptiste allowed it. He enjoyed the way some of those watching shifted with discomfort.

"You're not a worthy vessel," someone shouted from the back.

His gaze lasered on them, and a wolfish grin split his lips. "Says the runt who, back in the day, would have been abandoned in the woods for being weak. An error I shall rectify." His gaze then tracked the rest as he added in a low rumble, "You will regret following the false Alpha." And then he howled, a long and eerie sound that echoed through the forest.

His uncle's arrival ruined his chance at swaying any minds. Dressed in a long, velvet robe of midnight blue, Frederick uttered a loud rebuke. "Ignore my nephew and his last-ditch effort to save himself. He's proven himself unworthy over and over. Tonight, the Garou will be given a new host. One better suited for a god."

"I like this body." Garou kept talking through Baptiste's lips, and Uncle frowned.

"You'll like mine even more."

"As if I'd choose you," he sneered. "You are not worthy of carrying my essence."

"Stop pretending to speak with our god's voice."

"Foolish Freddie. Still so angry I didn't choose you," he mocked. "Do you know why I passed you over? Because I could see the weakness in your spirit."

Ruddy color blossomed in Uncle's cheeks. "Weak? Weak is my nephew who refuses to eat meat. Who won't step up and rule. Who whines and cries because someone died."

"Who has values that aren't swayed by peer pressure." Garou fixed those watching and listening wit ha stern gaze. "Who doesn't chase after power. Who shows remorse for something he couldn't control. All traits of a strong leader, unlike you. And worse, you can't even see it. As to the rest of you..." Garou's lip curled in a sneer. "Sheep. You're not worthy to call yourself wolves."

More and more of the pack looked away and swayed on their feet as if they wished to be anywhere else.

"Enough. Don't listen to my nephew. He's just pretending to speak for the Garou. Trying to sow doubt. Ignore him. He's babbling because he's afraid."

"More like exposing you for the weakling that you are. A true Alpha would challenge me, not bind me to a tree because he's a coward," Garou spat.

"You left me no choice. Running away. Refusing to do your duty. No more!" Frederick pulled a knife, the silver blade glinting as the last rays of the sunset struck it. "You won't escape this time. There is only one way forward, and it starts with your death."

To Baptiste's surprise, Diandra's father stepped forward. "While I grieve for my daughter, it was made very clear Baptiste was not in control at the time of her death. Evil magic was at play."

Frederick sneered. "What I do tonight has nothing to do with Diandra but everything to do with my nephew being unworthy to hold our god."

"You speak of unworthy and yet plan to kill him so ignobly?" Diandra's father waved a hand. "You have him bound in silver like a feral. It hardly seems fair or right. I think we should hold off and discuss this before doing something so extreme."

"There is nothing to discuss," Uncle barked. "I know what I'm doing. For years I've been seeking out a way to right this travesty, and finally, I came across the solution." Frederick held up the silver-coated blade. "Tonight, I shall make everything right."

Ask him who gave him the knife, Garou slyly whispered.

"Where did you get that dagger?" Baptiste asked. "Who told you to kill me?"

"I did." The feminine voice resolved into the shape of the witch he'd strangled only the day before. She sauntered into view, wearing an almost sheer white gown, her hair unbound and flowing down her back.

"Circe," Baptiste growled.

"Surprised to see me?" The witch stood straight, her head no longer at a broken angle.

"Who are you?" Uncle asked, annoyance creasing his features. "You're not allowed to be on Pack grounds."

"Is that any way to speak to the person who told you where to find your nephew?" Circe asked in mocked indignation.

"I've never met you before," Frederick declared.

"Not in person, no. But we had many conversations on the dark web. You had so many questions about how you could change the avatar holding your god."

"That was you?" Frederick gaped at Circe.

"Surprise!" Her feral smile sent a chill down Baptiste's spine.

Uncle blustered, "You lied to me. You're not one of us."

The revelation his uncle had colluded with Circe had Baptiste snapping, "You idiot. You've been taking advice from a witch who's been killing indiscriminately in an attempt to become a god."

"No." Frederick shook his head. "The person I spoke to claimed to be a scholar in Europe, a lone wolf who'd studied our kind and history."

Circe's laughter might sound like tinkling bells, but it sent an uneasy ripple through those watching and listening. "So gullible. The internet makes it so easy to fool people and you were easier than most, so desperate to take what was given to your nephew. So jealous your god didn't choose you. I have to admit, I never thought you'd go this far. Most people would balk at killing a close family member."

"You told me if I cut out his heart with this dagger and ate it while it still beat, I could capture the Garou's essence." Uncle dug his own grave with his admission and the vibe from those watching changed.

"You took advice from a witch?" Diandra's father spat.

Others in the pack shifted uneasily and murmurs arose that had Frederick's expression turning stony. "I didn't know. She misled me about her identity."

"I did," Circe admitted with a smile. "I never expected you'd be so gullible. No wonder your god passed you by. An avatar should be strong in conviction and character. But your weakness is to my benefit. Everyone is gathered, even your god. I couldn't have prepared this better, given what I have planned."

Frederick tried to save face by blustering, "Whatever it is you've plotted will fail. We will tear you to pieces."

"Blood will run this night, but I promise you, it won't

be mine. Ever heard the expression moon madness?" She didn't wait for a reply. "Do you know what causes it? I do. It's when the full moon rises, and the Pack shifts, but the Alpha dies, leaving them without a leader. The lack of an Alpha drives them to madness."

A pale Frederick gripped his silver knife tighter—which had to burn—and spat, "The only person dying tonight is you!"

"We'll see about that." She glanced at the sky. "The moon's almost here. Any last words?"

"Die, witch!" Uncle lunged with his silver knife, but Circe easily stepped aside.

She laughed. "How does it feel to know you're the reason why your entire pack is going to perish?"

For a second, Baptiste saw fear on Frederick's face. Then arrogance straightened Uncle's spine as the full moon appeared in the darkening sky. "You chose the wrong night to confront, witch." And with that threat, Uncle's face began to change, elongating into a muzzle, his limbs contorting, the flesh sprouting fur. The dagger fell to the ground as his fingers turned to paws.

Rather than look afraid, Circe clapped her hands. "How delightful. I could use a fur coat, and a rug, ooh, and a blanket." With that taunt the witch simply held up her hand and Uncle froze mid-shift, his body contorted and still standing on two legs. Circe bent and plucked the dagger from the ground. Before anyone realized her intent, she slashed it across Frederick's throat.

There was something horrifying about watching him bleed out, his eyes full of panic and fear. The man who'd tried to murder Baptiste shouldn't have deserved any sympathy, but Baptiste remembered the uncle who used to play football with him in the yard, who stood by his side when his father died and did his best to guide a young boy.

In the silence that followed the killing, the emerging moon struck the Pack standing still in shock. It changed them from men and women into wolves. Snarls filled the air as the beasts dropped into a low stance, readying to attack.

Circe's lips curved in amusement as she said, "Now the real fun begins."

CHAPTER 18

Daphne left the apartment with Nelly, Clive, and Marissa. They still didn't have a real plan because they had no idea what to expect other than wolves. Nelly and Clive did manage to borrow some sleep bombs from the SMU office across the street but had to do so furtively given their actions would be considered out of the scope of their employment.

Or as Clive said, "We're going somewhere we're not allowed to be and will have our asses reamed if caught."

Daphne admired the fact they didn't use that as an excuse to bail on Baptiste. It had been a long time since she had bothered to have friends. Her loss of her sisters in the grove made it difficult for her to allow anyone to get close. But it appeared time had healed that wound because look at her, collaborating with others, even planning for the future. When Nelly said, "I'll bet Baptiste's mom makes an awesome feast once we get him back home. Wait until you meet her. She's the best," it warmed her that Nelly assumed she'd be present. Even odder, she kind of looked forward to it.

But first, they had to rescue Baptiste.

They took a battered vehicle that Nelly claimed the SMU had confiscated from someone who'd thought to raid the Monster King's newly excavated palace. "Dumbass thought he could steal from a dude with literal monsters as his guards. It didn't end well for him. He's still not able to sleep, and he screams nonstop if they don't sedate him."

A god who didn't mess around. Daphne approved.

They ditched the junky car a half mile from the compound and continued on foot. The Mother had been mostly silent, her last words being: *Take care, Paladin. You are about to face your greatest challenge.* Some might have found that statement demoralizing, but Daphne never shied from a confrontation.

"Stay sharp. The compound property begins just beyond this bend in the road." Nelly indicated with a pointed finger. The main entrance was a mile past, but they didn't plan to enter that way.

Around the curve, they came in sight of a fence cleared of vegetation for several feet on either side. The barrier was metal, strands of it woven to make something called "chain link." Easy to climb. The sight of it had Daphne frowning. "I thought you said the area was secure."

"Don't let the benign appearance fool you," Nelly cautioned. "That fence is electrified and will knock you unconscious, maybe even stop your heart."

That explained the faint hum Daphne could hear. "How do we get past it?"

"Marissa and I will handle it. Rather than take out the power for the entire boundary which would warn those within we are coming, we're going to provide a bridge for the electricity, creating a dead spot in the fence that can be traversed." Clive glanced at the pink-haired witch. "Ready to block the current?"

The witch nodded and stood a few paces to Clive's left and raised her hands.

The moment Clive muttered, "Go!" Daphne and Nelly sprinted for the chain link, gripped the diamond-shaped holes, and quickly climbed. Daphne landed on the other side first, Nelly a few seconds after. Clive's expression took on an even more serious mien as he murmured, "Okay Marissa, your turn next. When I say go, climb over. Once you're on the other side, let me know when you're ready to grab the current from me."

Marissa nodded and her hands came down just as Clive said, "Go."

She vaulted for it, nimbly making her way over and immediately putting out her hands, expression taut. "I've got it. I think."

"So reassuring," Clive replied as he came to join them.

The moment he landed, Marissa let out a breath and huffed, "Damn, that's quite the electrical load they've got running through there."

"More than usual," Clive agreed. "Good thing it worked, or we'd have been barbecued."

"Mmm. I love barbecued meat." Daphne hummed.

When three sets of eyes stared at her she shrugged. "What? It's delicious."

Marissa snickered. "And to think you hooked up with a dude who doesn't eat any."

"Speaking of Baptiste, let's see what the Earth has to say about his location." She ducked down and placed her fingers on the ground, grimacing at its deadness. "I can't speak to the Mother. They've done something to block her access in this area."

"Is that going to be an issue?" Nelly asked.

"No. Unlike a witch, I don't have magic. Just me and my ability to fight." Nelly had supplied Daphne with an arsenal of new weapons. She had knives strapped to her body, more than she hoped to need. Baptiste might not be happy if she killed any of the wolves. At the same time, she wouldn't hesitate if it saved his life.

Marissa's lips turned down. "You're not the only one cut off. I can't access any extra magic either."

The reply had Clive pursing his lips. "I might be able to recharge you if you run out of magic, seeing as how my power isn't god-dependent." Apparently, the wizard had an innate ability to siphon off stray bits of magic. "Although, this area is a bit lacking in juice."

Nelly patted her holsters. "If the spells fail don't worry, I've got you covered."

"Remember, we're shooting to maim, not kill," Clive reminded. The wizard worried about starting a war with the wolves.

The wolves should be more worried about pissing off the Earth's Paladin. Daphne had the full blessing of the Mother to do what she had to. Mother even encouraged her before they'd left, saying, *Make haste, my daughter of the Earth, if you wish to save your mate.*

"I'm going to talk to some of the inhabitants." Daphne headed for a tree as Clive huffed, "We're supposed to avoid being seen."

"Wasn't talking about the two-legged kind," she muttered as she slapped her palm on the nearest tree. A shiver went through its trunk as she communicated with it, speaking aloud for her non-tree-understanding friends. "Where is Baptiste?" She projected an image of him for the poplar.

The tree's branches rattled.

"It doesn't know," she murmured. "Given its youth, its roots don't extend far enough to see anything of interest. We'll need to go deeper into the forest."

Clive glanced at the sky where the sun's final bright rays turned all kinds of colors. "We really need to get moving if we're going to snag Baptiste and get out before the wolves notice us."

"I thought the plan was to put any wolves we come across asleep," Daphne reminded as she set off in the direction her gut indicated.

"There's very little magic to play with on this side. Less than expected," Clive admitted. "Depending on how many shifted we encounter, that could pose an issue. They're more resistant to spells in their wolf shape."

Marissa trudged by her side. "If all else fails, climb a tree. That should keep us safe until morning."

Speaking of safe... Daphne's head canted as she heard a whisper in the boughs overhead. Her lips pursed at the news.

"We have a problem," she stated.

"What's wrong?" Nelly asked from her position ahead of them.

"Circe is here."

Marissa stumbled. "Wait, what? How?"

"I don't know, but that's just made the situation a lot more complicated." And dangerous for her companions.

"Are you sure?" Nelly asked.

"Trees don't know how to lie." Daphne pointed. "We'll need to split up. You guys go find Baptiste while I handle Circe."

"Handle her how?" Marissa pointedly asked. "Have you forgotten just how tricky and powerful she is?"

"I am aware," Daphne grumbled. "But what else can we do? If she's here, then someone has to distract her in case she's looking to mete out revenge on Baptiste for snapping her neck."

"We're stronger together," Nelly insisted.

Daphne would have argued, only the trees had more to say. "Seems like you'll get your wish. The ash says Circe is heading for Baptiste."

"Where exactly?" Clive queried.

"That way." Daphne pointed in the direction of the setting sun. "There's a very large oak in a clearing. They've tied Baptiste to it, and everyone has gathered around."

"How far is Circe from them?" Marissa asked.

"Not far." Daphne tried to filter the messages from the forest, the many rustling leaves, rubbing branches, and creaking limbs making it hard to separate. "We need to be careful, though. The fir trees are saying to watch for the rotted things."

"What's that supposed to mean?" Nelly's brow creased.

Daphne's shoulders rolled. "It's not quite clear. Their way of seeing things isn't the same as us."

"Whatever the threat, the plan stays the same. I'll scout ahead. Clive will flank to the left. Marissa, you bring up the back. If you see anything move, drop it with a sleep spell. If you can't, holler for me and I'll take it down with a non-lethal shot." Nelly reiterated their simple plot.

With that, they spread out, Nelly disappearing into the forest dappled with the last of the sunlight. Clive moved off to the side as Daphne kept walking straight, not needing the rub of leaves to know what direction to find Baptiste. She felt a tug, as if a vine stretched between them. She followed it, her steps silent, her resolve firm. She didn't know when she'd pulled her daggers, but they rested comfortably in her grip.

As she trod through the forest, the trees got quiet. No insects buzzed. A stench of rot filled the air.

The attack came suddenly, humps of leaves suddenly bursting into the air as bodies exploded from them.

"Zombies!" Nelly yelled.

Not quite. It took a second to grasp what attacked. Forest animals, but a grotesque version. The squirrel leaping for her was the size of a large dog, its eyes rolling in opposite directions, its flesh oozing with sores.

Daphne crossed her arms and slashed in an X that took the head off the flying rodent. It hit the ground, ichor leaking from the stump, the smell enough to make her eyes water.

To her left, Clive confronted something that once might have been a fox, but this one had an extra leg and a tail coming from its side. It drooled from its deformed jaw as it snapped. It froze when Clive flung magic at it.

"Kill it," Daphne advised. "We don't want it at our backs."

For a second, she thought he'd argue, but he held his finger out pointing at its head. The impact of the magic missile caved in its skull.

Marissa approached, huffing, "What the fuck? Zombie forest animals? I didn't realize Circe was a necromancer."

"She isn't," Daphne stated. "These animals were tainted by what she was doing outside Palusville. It would seem the fire didn't destroy everything."

"How many more can we expect?" Nelly asked as she neared, wiping her blades on a rag. Smart not using a gun as it would have been loud and announced their presence.

Daphne put a hand to a tree for answers. She bit her lip. "They can't give an exact number, but there are more."

"How did she get them into Nexus and past the Monster King?" Was Nelly's next question.

Clive replied, "I imagine she cloaked their arrival."

"Or the King ignored them, thinking them some of his subjects." Nelly's alternative answer. "Either way, we need to tread cautiously."

"But quickly. Baptiste is in trouble." Daphne could

feel his emotions, the anger. The frustration of being caught.

It led to her suddenly running, fleet of foot and graceful as she leapt and bounded through the forest, following the invisible tether. Her companions tried to follow but couldn't keep up.

The forest darkened as twilight took hold. The full moon rose, but the gleam didn't penetrate this section of the woods. A howl erupted. Then another.

Close.

Almost there.

Seeing lights up ahead, she didn't slow down but rather burst into a clearing lit with torches spaced around the open area. They illuminated the chaotic scene. Wolves, all shapes and colors, fought with each other, snarling and snapping, their eyes wild with madness.

A woman watched. Circe, healed of her injury, stood tall over a prone body on the ground, lying in a pool of blood.

But the thing that drew Daphne's eye? The massive tree taking the place of pride. Bound to it in silver was her beast, who looked straight at her as if he'd known she was coming.

She waggled her fingers and he hissed, "What the fuck, Psycho? Get out of here."

"I don't think so. You owe me breakfast." She spoke to him but kept her gaze on Circe, the most dangerous one in the group. "And once I save you, I expect to be fed promptly."

He groaned. "Now is not the time for humor."

"Wasn't being funny. I'm actually kind of annoyed. Your uncle had no right to kidnap you."

Circe turned to see her talking to Baptiste and smirked. "Well, well, if it isn't the dryad. I'm surprised to see you here. Haven't you heard? The wolves don't like people trespassing on their grounds."

"Yet here you are. I'm surprised the wolves haven't tried to eat you yet. Then again, old and stringy meat probably isn't high on their list."

Rather than react to the barb, Circe waved a hand. "They're a little too busy attacking each other. Moon madness caused by the death of their Alpha." She glanced at the body at her feet. "Not a very good one, I should add."

On that, they agreed. "I don't suppose you'll save me the exertion and just let me cut off your head?" Daphne asked nicely.

Circe smiled back just as cattily. "It's like you want me to curse you again. But lucky for you, you're more useful to me dead."

"You should know by now I'm not that easy to kill."

"Says the dryad who entered a place where the Mother can't reach."

"Shows how little you know." Her lips tilted. "Looks to me like I'm still standing on Earth surrounded by trees, making this part of the Mother's kingdom."

"Your goddess has no power here," Circe insisted.

"Is that what you think?" Daphne lied and kept smiling as her slow movements brought her to stand between Baptiste and Circe.

"I'm going to enjoy cracking open your chest and

eating your heart. And then I'll ingest that of the Garou, making him a part of me."

"You know, I like meat. Love it, actually, but even I have lines I don't cross. Cannibalism is one of them."

Her comment met with a snicker from Baptiste and a murmured, "I don't know, I kind of like eating you."

A startling thing to hear in the situation, but it oddly made her bolder.

Circe pursed her lips. "You're missing out. Humans have the most tender meat, especially the young ones. Their souls are also especially juicy in power and, lucky me, these dumb dogs collected them all in one place for an easy slaughter."

"Don't you dare touch the children," Baptiste growled.

"Or what? You're not in a position to make any demands and neither is your tree bitch. By the time dawn arrives, you'll all be dead. Your souls will make a great contribution to my new well of power. Thanks to your actions, I've decided I won't waste my time on puny humans anymore."

"You're a complete and utter lunatic," Daphne murmured.

"Says the soon to be kindling," Circe spat back.

Before the last syllable left the witch's lips, Daphne's knife flew but her target moved fast enough to avoid being impaled in the heart. Circe only suffered a nicked arm.

The scratch curled Circe's lip. "My turn." She flung a spell from her hand at Daphne, the ball of fire a sizzling blue. Daphne wondered if the drain on magic in this area would affect her too. Only one way to find out. She needed to force the witch to use her power in the hopes it ran out.

Daphne used a poignard with a repelling spell to block it along with Circe's next tossed attack. Before Circe could throw a third, Daphne fired several small knives, one after another, pulling them from her chest harness and whipping them at her enemy.

The witch threw up a shield and uttered a low sound of irritation. "You're so annoying. Let's see how you do against a pack of rabid wolves." Circe's next flung spell wasn't at Daphne but towards the furballs fighting amongst themselves.

As one, they suddenly stopped their furry fighting and their shaggy heads swiveled. Glowing eyes, too many of them, fixated on Daphne. One of the wolves uttered a low growl and stepped forward. Then another.

Baptiste yelled, "Leave her alone! She's not the enemy."

But the wolves weren't listening and there were too many for Daphne to stand and fight.

"I'll be back for you," she promised as she sprinted for the forest. The trees whispered of a spot where she could take a stand.

First, though, she had to make it.

CHAPTER 19

Daphne bolted with a pack of wild wolves hot on her heels. Meanwhile, Circe remained, looking all too smug. She glanced at Baptiste and smirked. "Guess no one's coming to save you."

Fuck his life. He was more concerned about Daphne.

Circe grabbed the dagger she'd used to slit his uncle's throat and sauntered closer. "It's amazing to me how greed blinds people. Look at your uncle. He was so desperate to take what you have that he listened to a stranger."

"You won't get away with this."

"I already have." She waved a hand to show the bodies of the wolves felled already by the moon madness. A few might recover, but the trauma of what they'd done would linger.

He would know, given he'd done a terrible thing not of his choosing. A memory that would live on forever. "Your plan will fail."

"Seems to me like it's going quite well, actually."

Stop wasting time chatting with the witch and do something, Garou admonished. *Our mate will die if you don't.*

Exactly what could he do? He remained fucking bound in silver. No amount of straining loosened the chains, and he doubted Circe would set him free.

She ran the tip of the dagger against his chest. "One thing I didn't lie to your uncle about? Eating your heart will pass on the Garou god's essence."

No, it won't. I'd rather let this part of me die than join with that witch.

The bullet that struck Circe in the chest took them both by surprise. She glanced at the hole and screeched even as a second bullet came flying.

It struck a rapidly erected magic shield and missed its mark, but that didn't stop Nelly from exiting the woods and firing nonstop, each impact making Circe retreat a step. A fireball came shooting from the forest as well.

They're forcing her to use magic in the hopes she runs out.

Baptiste didn't question how Garou knew. He watched as Clive emerged from the woods to join Nelly, hands upraised and glowing. He was joined by Marissa. Together, they flung a large electrical ball at the witch who hissed before whirling to run.

His friends took off after her rather than take the time to free him. In their defense, they had no idea Daphne was in grave peril and went after what they deemed the greatest threat.

Since they're busy, we'd better go and save her. Time to break free. Now that the moon is up, we can use it to our advantage.

Use it how? The silver prevented the shift.

In ordinary wolves. But we are more than that. You have the essence of a god running through you, and the full moon puts us at our strongest. Add to that, our mate is in danger, our Pack is being destroyed, and the pups will be slaughtered unless we act.

He wanted to do something. He wanted to save them all.

Then be angry. Be the Alpha they want. Be the protector they need. Be the mate she deserves. Accept what you are.

Hadn't he done that already?

No.

And it wasn't Garou that shattered that lie. He'd spent his life trying to be something more than an avatar. He wanted people to respect him for the things he did not because he carried part of a deity within.

And they do. Haven't you noticed? They don't respect you because of me. They respect you because of the example you set.

What respect? His own people left him bound.

Out of fear. Your uncle is gone now, though. You can show them a different way. But you don't have much time.

Garou was right. He couldn't afford to fight his other side, not with so much at stake. Baptiste closed his eyes and took deep breaths. The moonlight bathed his skin and tingled. The silver still burned, but he took that pain and shoved it aside. So what if it hurt? Many things hurt. Using that pain, overcoming it, made a person stronger.

In that moment, as the pain of it disappeared, it hit him. How could silver, a common metal, bind a god?

It can't. It's your own belief that's holding you back.

Because he refused to accept.

No longer.

He huffed and pulled deep within, tugged at the primal part of him that he liked to keep separate, but which remained wound around the very core of him. Time to join them and stop pretending he wasn't special.

I am the avatar of a god. It's time I acted like one.

With that realization he tilted his face to the moon, the full glow enhancing his innate power. With his acceptance, change ripped through him. The sudden bulk broke the chains that he'd been foolish enough to believe could hold him. He roared as he finished shifting, sprouting course fur and sharp claws, but the best part? His senses magnified.

There were two scents that interested, one being that of the witch he hated, but the more important one? That of his mate, being chased and in danger.

He went on a loping run, his long stride eating up the forest floor as he raced for her. Through their bond, he felt her annoyance—not fear or pain. How like her. At the same time, he sensed her exertion as she fought off those that attacked.

Luckily, she'd not gone far, but managed to put herself in a precarious place. She stood on the edge of a ravine, the bottom of it a rough landing since the creek only ran high in the spring. Daphne danced on that dangerous edge, arms whipping out like vines to wrap around a snapping wolf and toss it into the forest, bending almost in half as another leapt for her throat. The wolf missed and would have plummeted, but she shot a hand to grab it and slow its fall.

Even in deadly danger, she tried to not kill, and he knew why.

Because she knows it's my Pack.

At seeing how she thought of others before herself, he howled, a strident sound that startled the wolves into halting their attack. They whirled and stared as Baptiste stomped in their direction, seething and glaring, his displeasure clear.

Faced with an Alpha who was also part god, they bowed. Front legs folded. Bellies dipped to touch the earth. They crawled to him and whined, begging for his forgiveness.

He growled. *Do not touch my mate.*

They whimpered but obeyed, except for the same cocky bastard whose scent he'd identified before. That wolf dared to lift his head. Baptiste made an example of him. He grabbed the wolf by the scruff and threw him into the ravine.

The wolves remained plastered to the ground as he strode past them for his woman, who cocked her head and said, "Hey, Beast. About time you joined the party."

His voice emerged in a low guttural growl, "Sorry I'm late."

Her lips quirked. "At least you didn't miss all the fun. Where's Circe?"

"Being chased by our friends."

"In that case, we should go help them. Care to lead the way?"

"Follow me." As he began loping, Daphne kept pace by his side and the Pack fell in behind them.

In short order they found their friends holed up in a

tree, the base of which had a dozen wolves pacing around it and another handful lying on the ground snuffling with sleep. The moment they scented Baptiste, the wolves whirled, but whatever snarl they started to emit got choked as they recognized him. Bodies hit the ground and crawled, the moon madness leaving them as their god-Alpha straightened out their minds.

Daphne paid the whining wolves no mind as she stepped through them to reach the base of the maple tree. She patted its trunk. "Thanks for keeping them safe."

The branches quivered.

His mate glanced upward. "You can come down now."

"We lost Circe!" Nelly grumbled. "She sent some of those mutant forest animals after us, and then next thing we knew, the wolves were on our asses, so we climbed."

Clive grimaced as he hit the ground. "I actually ran out of magic. This place is remarkably bereft."

"No shit," Marissa huffed. "I've not been this weak since that time I went on a cruise and had to fend off a kraken attack."

While Baptiste's friends stiffened and warily watched his approach, Daphne didn't flinch when he put his paw-like hand on her shoulder. In a low rumble, he stated, "These woods are safe now. The Pack recognizes you as friends."

"I wouldn't say safe quite yet," Marissa remarked, nimbly leaping down. "If your Pack is in the mood to hunt something, send them after Circe's mutants. They're all over the forest."

He glanced at Gordy, one of the older pack members. "Find the intruders."

A mottle-furred Gordy dipped his head before yipping to the others.

Before they all ran off, Daphne interjected, "Don't send all of them. Some of the wolves should check on those felled by the mighty oak, and we need to protect the children."

"I'm almost out of magic, but I can still fire a gun, so I'll go," Marissa volunteered.

Nelly shoved at Clive. "You're out of juice too. Take this and go with her." She handed him a revolver. Some men might have argued, but Clive had always had the greatest respect for Nelly, a fighter who didn't need a man to protect her.

As the wolves and the magic users moved off, Daphne flipped back her wild mane of hair and with eyes gleaming said, "Time put an end to a witch."

He couldn't help a wolfish grin that turned into a howl that filled the sky.

Time to hunt.

CHAPTER 20

DAPHNE HAD NEVER HUNTED WITH SOMEONE BEFORE, AND despite the danger, there was a certain playful excitement to it. As she raced through the forest, her fleet feet always finding purchase, he kept pace. A bigger, lumbering shape that nonetheless had a grace to his motions.

Poor Nelly couldn't keep up, but they didn't dare slow. Circe couldn't be allowed to escape.

The trees helped her by rustling to show her the path taken by the witch. A good thing, since Baptiste growled, "She's masked her scent."

But Circe couldn't hide her flight. The forest knew what she'd done in Palusville and understood if allowed to go free, she'd spew her poison again.

Mutants tried to guard Circe's retreat, their misshapen bodies plummeting suddenly from trees and bursting from the ground. They even popped out from behind wide trunks.

Daphne barely paused. She slashed with her daggers

and kept going. Baptiste roared as he swung and handled those who dared get too close. A distant pop let her know Nelly remained on their heels.

The forest thinned as the rocky ground began to rise, the slope of it turning steep and forcing her to crane, looking upward in time to see a floating Circe alight atop the bluff. The witch stood with arms outstretched while a brisk gust of wind whipped around her, whirling through her hair. She shot a few lightning bolts into the sky and Daphne didn't understand why until she heard something caw in the distance.

"Too late," Circe cackled, catching sight of Daphne who had begun to ascend. "Here comes my ride."

While a fast climber, Daphne knew she would never reach the witch in time because the second cry from the animal she'd called sounded much closer. She couldn't let her get away. Not after all she'd done. Not considering all she'd do.

I have to stop her.

The trees atop the bluff, few and scraggly as they were, swayed in the breeze that tugged at Circe's hair. They gave Daphne an idea. The Mother might not be present, but Daphne was. A dryad who'd once been a sapling but became something more. A fighter. A survivor. A Paladin in charge of Earth's defense.

And people in charge were supposed to give orders.

Daphne braced herself on a ledge, opened her arms wide, and shouted, "Brothers and sisters of the seed and root. I command you in the Mother's name. I beseech you on behalf of those the witch tortured. Help me to stop a grave evil."

The forest all around went still as the trees listened.

A suddenly nervous Circe sputtered, "There's nothing you can do."

"Is that so? Let's find out shall we." Daphne smiled as she said, "Mulch her."

The boughs closest to Circe reached out with spindly tips that tangled in her hair. Circe exclaimed and slapped at them, huffing, "I don't think so. Burn, you fucking twigs."

The witch ignited the limbs touching her, their dry bark making them burst into bright flames, but that didn't stop the trees from fighting. Roots shot up from the ground and wrapped around the witch's ankles, yanking her down before she could scream. More wiggling tendrils emerged to whip around her body, binding her arms tight, covering her mouth, immobilizing her, and stifling what remained of her magic.

Daphne didn't startle when a tree at her back slid a branch around her waist and lifted, elongating and bending that it might deposit the dryad atop the bluff to stand by the bound witch. Daphne knelt by Circe, whose wide eyes could do nothing but blink in fear. Good. It had been a long time in coming. At the same time, Daphne knew better than to think the witch would repent. Some evils would never change.

And so she whispered, "We are all part of the Earth and when we die, we return to it." Nourishing the next generation.

The roots tightened, cutting through flesh, snapping bone until all that remained were bloody bits. The ground then swallowed them. By the time Daphne stood, all that remained of Circe was a damp spot in the dirt.

"Remind me to not piss you off," Baptiste murmured in his deep beast voice as he clambered over the edge to join her.

"Then you'd better feed me. I'm starving after all that work." Daphne whirled to smile at him just as something big swooped overhead. Before she could look up to see, a gunshot cracked and the giant bird came tumbling down. A glance below showed Nelly lowering her gun.

"About time I got to kill something," Nelly complained. "Now, if we're done fighting bad guys, I could use a beer, a pizza, and a shower, in that order."

Daphne clapped her hands. "That sounds like an excellent plan."

However, Baptiste grunted and through their bond, she sensed why. She put a hand on his hairy arm. "You should join your pack and make sure the forest is cleansed of threats. I'll see you at dawn."

A toothy grin and a pat on her butt were his thanks before he bounded off, practically leaping from the bluff to the ground. As he ran into the woods, his shape shifted from two-legged to four, and he howled, a cry answered by the other wolves in the forest.

Daphne joined Nelly and said, "Nice shot," before she kicked at the feathered creature large enough to carry a person in flight. "What is it?"

"Rukh. Kind of rare, meaning we should probably get rid of it before someone notifies the Cryptid Preservation Society and gives me shit for taking it down. Think you can get your tree friends to mulch it like Circe?"

"Seems like a waste." Daphne pursed her lips. "How's it taste barbecued?"

Delicious as it turned out. Baptiste and his Pack found them on the back patio of the pack compound, using the massive firepit to cook the bird on a spit. Only part of what they'd done while they waited for the night to end. The injured had been taken care of and the dead readied for burial. Meanwhile, the children had slept through the entire affair.

Despite the events of the night, there was jubilance as the Pack and their new Alpha expanded the barbecued bird to include eggs, fruit, and pancakes. The children woke and joined them, adding laughter and exuberance to the mix. It was the biggest party Daphne had ever attended and intimidating as well, hence why she snuck off and climbed the nearest tree, a lilac that told her she should come back in the spring to smell her blooms.

Her disappearance didn't go unnoticed. Baptiste tracked her movements and kept an eye out as the Pack approached and apologized for their actions. He tolerated it only for a little bit before he suddenly stood and declared, "I'm going to bed." Which apparently meant she was supposed to go with him, seeing as how he headed for her tree. She slipped out of its welcoming branches only to gasp as he tossed her over his shoulder and began stomping for the main house.

"I can walk," she remarked.

"Yeah, but the whole caveman act is a tradition among the newly mated."

"About the mating thing..."

"I'm sorry I didn't ask or warn you first. In my

defense, I didn't know that would happen without a bite."

"Fair enough. What does it mean, though?"

"We're basically married," he stated.

Daphne stiffened in his arms. Married?

CHAPTER 21

Baptiste felt Daphne's body tighten and he paused before he crossed the threshold into the Pack house.

"Are you mad?" He flipped her to a cradled position in his arms so he could see her face.

"Surprisingly enough, no. It would seem I'm kind of fond of you." Her arms laced around his neck.

"Just fond? Guess I'll have to work worker harder to ensure you love me."

Her lips curved. "I don't think it will take much convincing, but I will note that being mated doesn't negate the fact I am still the Mother's champion."

"Good. Because I'd hate for you to change. I like you just the way you are," he said as he bounded up some stairs. "Actually, that's not entirely true." He set her on her feet inside the bedroom he used when he stayed overnight at the compound.

She planted her hands on her hips. "Meaning what? What about me don't you like?"

"The amount of clothes you're still wearing," he

stated with a wink.

A problem quickly rectified. His robe hit the floor almost as fast as she stripped.

He uttered a low rumble at the sight of her. The swell of her hips, the indent of her waist, her firm breasts topped with berries. Perfection, and every inch his. And he would claim it. He intended to lick, caress, and discover every inch of her. To imprint himself upon her smooth and sexy skin. To fill her with his seed and make her scream in delight.

He dragged her to him for a kiss, but she didn't let him taste her lips for long. She reached between their bodies to put a hand on his shaft, making him gasp as she squeezed. "Sit," she commanded, pushing him to a chair. He sat and she knelt between his legs, still gripping his cock, her tight grip sliding back and forth.

"Shouldn't I be the one between your legs?" he complained.

"No. Now, be quiet," said as she took him into her mouth.

And he wasn't talking about just the tip. She went all the way to the root of him, which had never happened before. Somehow, she managed and, even better, sucked at his flesh while doing it. The intense sensation just about had him exploding.

Teeth gritted, he held on to the arms of the chair as she suctioned his length, dragging him to the brink. As if sensing he'd spill too quickly, she stopped and teased him, licking him up and down, swirling her tongue around the swollen tip, even nibbled the flesh, making him gasp.

He'd never experienced anything like it, and while he was tempted to blow his load, he wanted this first time with them being officially mated to happen inside her.

"Come here," he growled, tugging her upwards.

"But I wasn't done," she complained even as she obeyed, but slowly, kissing her way up his body until she reached his lips.

He dragged her into his lap, the skin-to-skin touch not only electrifying but satisfying. She suited him like he would have never imagined. Aroused him like no other. He broke the kiss to taste her, sucking at the flesh of her neck, teasing the lobe of her ear which had her squirming in his lap in a good way.

The chair was wide enough that he could maneuver her around to straddle him properly. She sat on her haunches, her hand once more on his dick, rubbing the head of it against her moist core.

It would have been so easy to slip into her and fuck.

But the scent of her…

He suddenly grabbed her around the waist and stood.

"What are you doing?" she pouted.

"You'll see." He tossed her onto the bed, and she bounced, her legs splaying apart displaying pink perfection.

"My turn," he growled, kneeling between her legs. He leaned in close and rubbed the edge of his jaw against the soft skin of her inner thigh. A shiver went through her body. He kept rubbing, teasing her with the scrape of his unshaven jaw, blowing hotly on her. Every sound she made, her scent, the moisture that glistened, made him harder.

"Stop teasing," she huffed, wiggling her hips.

"Says the woman who started the teasing." Words spoken against her flesh before licked. Her hips arched and a soft cry emerged from her.

Pleased at her reactions, he licked her again and again, humming as he tasted her sweet nectar. He pulsed with need. He wanted nothing more than to slide into her velvety sheath but not until he had her squirming.

He feasted on her, lapping between her parted lips, toying with her clit, flicking and rubbing it. She writhed and moaned at his touch. Her hips pushed against his face, her ragged pants music to his ears.

His tongue speared into her, and she did her best to clench it, and mewled when it wasn't enough. He thrust two fingers into her, and she sighed as she clamped on his digits as they reached that sweet inner spot. He kept tonguing her clit while his fingers pumped, and he was rewarded with a sharp cry as she came, her channel pulsing and squeezing so tight his cock jerked in response.

He slid into her while she was still quivering, his cock straining to go deep. He thrust into her, striking her sweet spot harder than his fingers could. The friction of their bodies brought her to the peak again, and she gasped and clawed at him. Her hips rolled in demand. Her pussy clenched him tight.

It was almost too much. He wanted to come so bad but staring down into her flushed face he first growled, "Open your eyes."

She did, and they shone with passion. Her lips parted as she murmured, "My beast."

Yes, hers.

He thrust over and over into her, reveling in her tight, wet heat and in the way she gasped each time he hit her g-spot.

With their gazes locked, they rocked and found a rhythm, one that had them both tightening. He ground into her and circled his hips, pushing his cock deep into her over and over until she clenched so tight, he couldn't move.

And then she came, her climax hitting first with a vise-like grip, then rippling in waves that drew his own orgasm. He spilled inside her, still staring into her soul through her eyes. Seeing her, like she saw him.

Two people who'd been through so much on their journey to finally finding each other.

Finding a way forward.

Deserving of happiness.

They spent that morning in bed, napping in a tangle, waking to make love again. They left the compound late in the afternoon because while he might be Alpha, this wasn't yet his home. Not to mention, Daphne still couldn't connect to the Mother. Something he'd have to change if they were going to live there.

The moment they set foot outside the gate, the Mother spoke, and he heard as she said, *I am glad to see you victorious, my champion, and receiving your much deserved happily ever after.*

Then a message just for him. *Hurt her and I will turn you into fertilizer.*

EPILOGUE

The following spring...

A content Baptiste lounged on the back patio, relaxing with a beer. Much had happened since he'd taken over the Pack. For one, the compound had the totems blocking the Mother removed so she could talk to her favorite paladin. Two, the Pack learned real quick he wasn't his uncle. He abolished all kinds of old rules relating to arranged marriages to preserve bloodlines. Part of his amends to Diandra. Some of the Pack didn't agree and left, but they were outnumbered by those who journeyed to find and join the pack with the progressive Alpha who carried a piece of their god.

The voice of the Garou hadn't been heard since that eventful night when they'd finally become one whole being. It hadn't changed Baptiste much. He remained mostly the same but for his raunchier sense of humor. It led to him saying things like, "Bend over a little bit more," to his mate who wore some very short, shorts.

Daphne cast him a glare over her shoulder. "You know, instead of ogling my butt, you could be helping."

He spread his hands and grinned. "We both know I have a hairy thumb."

"But you can wield a shovel," she groused.

"I would offer but the last time I asked if you needed help you threatened to cut off my balls." Apparently, offering to carry in groceries was a crime. "Besides, you were the one who said you wanted a garden."

"I do. There is something very satisfying about nurturing a seed until it grows and blossoms into a living thing."

"If you say so. I think I'll stick to growling at people and running around on the full moon."

"Don't forget peeing on things," she reminded.

"Very important," he agreed solemnly.

"Pee on my garden and I will rip it off though," she sweetly promised.

To which he laughed. "I will let the Pack know."

"Oh, speaking of seeds, I'm going to need your help with one." She rose and dusted off her hands.

"I thought we just agreed the garden was your thing."

"Well, since you're the one who planted this one, I kind of figured you'd want a hand in cultivating it," she said with a coy smile.

It took him a second and then his jaw dropped. His gaze went to her belly. His brain misfired before he stammered, "You're pregnant?"

"Don't look so surprised. It was bound to happen given how often we have sex." She grabbed his hand and placed it on her abdomen. "Oh, and as a thank you from the Mother, she's blessed my womb with twins."

"Twins..." He suddenly felt faint and wavered on his feet.

His not-so-gentle mate slapped him.

He blinked.

She smiled. "You're welcome."

He laughed. A thing he thought he'd never do again until he found someone who showed him that even after adversity it was okay to live and love again.

He grabbed her around the waist and swung her until she gasped, "You're going to wear my lunch if you don't stop."

A good enough reason to set her on her feet and give her a long kiss. "I love you, Psycho." More than he could have ever imagined.

Being Daphne, she sassed, "I love you more, my beast. Now feed me. The babies are hungry."

In the next state over...

In the months since Marissa's return from her sojourn in Nexus, her Cryptid Authority office transformed. Given the previous boss's misdoings with Circe, management had been replaced. Ralph had also finally been fired and last she heard, worked as a security guard for some auto parts place.

Since they were short-staffed, Marissa had been working solo, which she enjoyed. No one to mess up her car or get in her way. Alas, when she accidentally destroys some private property while securing a cryptid, her new boss suddenly decides she needs a babysitter. His name? Koda Whiteclaw. A CA celebrity super-agent and go-to problem solver, who also happens to be an attractive man with a tanned complexion, grayish-white hair, and a body to drool over.

Seduction will have to wait, though, as they'll be entangled in a mystery that will threaten her life while also shedding light on her mysterious past.

Read all about Marissa's adventure—and romance!—in *Earth's Secret*.

www.ingramcontent.com/pod-product-compliance
Lightning Source LLC
LaVergne TN
LVHW031540060526
838200LV00056B/4587